ARMISTICE

ARMISTICE

A Love Story

Peter Abbot

Rock's Mills Press
Oakville, Ontario
2020

Published by
Rock's Mills Press
www.rocksmillspress.com

Cover image: "The Battle of Britain" by Paul Nash (1889–1946).

For information, please contact Rock's Mills Press at customer.service@rocksmillspress.com

And so we drifted twenty years
down the stream of time
feeling that such a storm
could not break again.
(Herbert Read, "Ode Written during the Battle of Dunkirk",
Collected Poems, 1946)

For the second time within a generation, worldwide calamity has
descended upon us.... *Sursum corda.*
Let us keep our heads and lift up our hearts!
(Vera Brittain, "Lift up your Hearts", *Peace News,* 8 September 1939)

I have nothing to offer but blood, toil, tears, and sweat....We have
before us many, many long months of struggle and of suffering.
(Winston Churchill, First Speech as Prime Minister, 13 May 1940)

15 Steel Road
Hamilton, Ontario
Canada

6 July 1939

Dear Margaret,

*You will be surprised to have a letter from me – after so long, and after we parted in such anger and resentment (at least **I** did) (to my shame) – can it be nearly twenty years ago? Yes, almost that, it was near the end of that War, the one that was going to end all wars. And yet here we are again, heading for another one, that's what our newspapers are saying – and maybe even worse if that's possible - my Father in his last letter (dictated) said that. It seems hideous after all the good intentions, all the hopes, all those Never-agains – do you know that Sassoon poem "Swear that you'll never forget"?? - and yet the whole world seems to have forgotten.*

But I'm getting a long way ahead of myself. You'll be thinking I'm still that odd gawky Canadian girl you invited to tea one day and then couldn't get rid of! I still feel ashamed – I was so rude, so immature, how did you ever have any time for me at all?? But you did, Margaret. I have never thanked you enough for your kindness to a troubled and troublesome stranger (as I sure was when we first met, and afterwards). Maybe it's too late for me now – even to apologize - yes, and please believe I'm being serious – especially, now at last, to thank you for your kindness, all your kindness.

Can you bear to see me again? I hope I'm a bit more mature than that silly girl you befriended – you and all your family – How are they? Will must be in his late-thirties now, and even the girls will be over 30!! Where have the years gone???

But I haven't told you why I'm returning to England (especially when everything looks so dark and threatening everywhere one looks and getting worse all the time, Hitler and Mussolini etc) - So why am I coming over now? It's for several reasons, starting with Daddy. You may remember he's why I was in England before, he and Mummy had separated and she had taken me with her back to Canada, and then I had a fight with Mummy and her boyfriend and Daddy sent money for me to visit him in London in 1913 – and then of course the war started and nurses were needed urgently.

Oh, it's all complicated, and long ago, and then Daddy remarried and his wife didn't want me, I think, Hilda, and after that - But he's very sick now, in hospital, heart-disease - and he wrote me and said he wants to see me before he dies - And Barry died last year, I don't think you ever met him but you may remember me telling you about him, my cousin, he was the Canadian soldier I married, he was wounded at the Battle of Passchendaele and blinded, and I nursed him and then he begged me to marry him? - and so I did - (I think you knew about that – but maybe you didn't? - it was such a confusing time, everything so painful and intense, and I just wanted to do something good with my life, I wanted to be helpful, and he had suffered so much -)

But it's hard to explain all this, especially in a short letter, after so long - If we do get together, maybe it will be easier (if you even want to, I mean), to catch up – And of course I hope you will tell me so much about yourself and your lives, I would really like that.

I think I should end off now. With all my love to you, Margaret, and the children – well, they're not children now, of course – Will and Jane and Emily -

Sincerely,
Ann

Crab-apple Cottage, Edge

Oh Ann!!!
When I saw your handwriting on the envelop my knees almost gave way I had to sit down it was in the Market & I had just sold the last of last year's apples when Jane ran over from the PO waving your letter, she recognised your writing too, of course she would, even after so long, & from Canada, & she's a librarian now – but she comes most weekends to help me, & Emily does too, they take turns -
But I'm gabbling – like you always said YOU did!!! What does that say – it says we must have a good long talk, several good long talks, ASAP. There's so much to catch up, isn't there, so much we'll talk about – so COME

– yes come as soon as possible, my dear. Just send me the details – which ship you'll be traveling on? - & especialy which train or bus to here – when you can visit us, I mean, after seeing your Father - & what your plans are – once you have seen your Father & are free to come down here to spend some time with us? The girls still talk about you, & all the walks you did together, & the flowers & birds, & the games you played with them - & Will, you wont recognise him – he lives in London - & I have two grandchildren, Emily's two children, Michael who is six & Oliver, four – my lovely grandchildren.

So, dear Ann, just come! Come! COME! We'll all be waiting to welcome you. COME!!!

Meg

One

'Margaret, is that you? I can hardly hear you – this seems to be a bad line – What? Yes, yes, it *is* me - Ann - yes it's *Ann*. I'm in London, I'm telephoning from a call-box outside the Hospital, or trying to – Yes, I've been with Daddy ever since I arrived, he's – I'll tell you all about it later – and about our ship nearly being sunk, did you hear about that? We were lucky to survive, but that's a long story – and I guess top secret, nobody seems to have heard about it. He's not good, Daddy, but we have had time together and some good talks and his Doctor says he needs relaxation now, he was getting too excited, his blood-pressure was up - I remember that's how it was with Barry - and I could – Yes, yes - his doctor said I could safely be away for a few days, Hilda's with him some of the time - So I wondered about this weekend – I gave them your phone number, at the Hospital I mean, hope you don't mind, so if I come, they can contact me to tell me if I should – if he - yes – Oh, that's good, that's wonderful - I'll get to you by tomorrow afternoon – yes, by train – Don't stay in for me, I still know my way, I think, from Street Station – some things you don't forget - No, please – I'll be all right - So, see you tomorrow – my love to you all – 'Bye for now.'

Meg put down the 'phone, thinking Yes, that's Ann, that same helter-skelter gabble, but maybe it was also because the line was bad and she couldn't hear what I was trying to say – and it's quite a while since her letter, so I was wondering if she still - But do I really want her back in our lives? even very temporarily? At first I was excited, optimistic, just hearing from her after all this time – her letter, out of the blue - but then, after all that happened in the past – and I did reply immediately, I did tell her she'd be welcome. Maybe I was taken by surprise, not remembering, then – not thinking, then, about all the other things, all the sadness – and the anger – all that I've been remembering since then. And what will the children think about it? That wasn't in my mind at all, when I replied, I should have waited a few days - too impulsive, that's me. Always too impulsive. And Jane will have told Emily, I'd better ring them both tonight - and Will too. But at the very least it will be interesting to see Ann again. Whatever her faults, she was such a lively young woman – And of course she was beautiful – tall, slim, fair hair, big green eyes, big smile – very fit, she loved walking in the countryside, and she and the children loved playing together, Jane and Emily adored her – and Davey, well, -

Meg finished her interrupted supper, then washed up the pots and cutlery, glancing occasionally through the kitchen window at the path winding up towards her - winding up past the apple-trees, and then on towards the cottage – The path up which Ann came into our lives - yes and I saw her, with Davey carrying her rucksack - I was standing right here, wasn't I? Yes, and that old apple-tree, the one that was blown down in the Big Storm - 1925, wasn't it? - the big old apple-tree beside the path - where I also saw them, sometime later, in the last light of the sun, standing so close to each other, one summer evening, how many years ago – both standing there, under the apple-tree. I can still see them, in my memory - and even from here I could see her rapt expression – and then he reached up and picked an apple and gave it to her, and then he kissed her – on her forehead, not her mouth - but still it was a shock, seeing that – And was that when hostility, even anger, began? – with her and especially with Davey - but I think it was mainly confusion I felt – at that time - Did that moment change everything for all three of us? Maybe. Yes, I think it did. And also for the children? Yes, maybe – But don't just stand here, there's work to do, Old Woman - the chickens and sheep still to feed, and Elsie, and Horace, and it's getting late. So get moving, get moving, Old Woman!

She stopped to look at herself in the mirror hanging near the front door; smoothed down her hair, grimacing – What an old woman you are, Margaret Avery! – so many wrinkles, such a leathery skin, and that scrawny neck, and thinning grey hair - but at least my eyes still do their job quite well – and my arms and legs too. I wonder how time has treated Ann – I always thought she was so beautiful – so beautiful and so natural, so self-confident – so *young*. So Canadian! Well, get on now, Meg - the chickens and sheep are waiting.

Two

Ann, carrying a small suitcase, arrives at Street Station, and sets off by foot for Edge.

It's a fine dry late-summer afternoon. A few yellow leaves lie crushed on the road, and occasionally others flutter down daintily beside her.

She is surprised when an old black car stops at the side of the road just ahead of her, and an elderly man steps out of it. He is wearing a shabby cap, which he doffs, and equally shabby jacket and trousers. 'Miss' he says. 'Remember me? William Fortune?'

Yes, she does. Of course she does. Owner of the small local garage and cafe; part-time local taxi-driver.

'Oh, Mr Fortune – yes, I do, but how can you – and after so many years - ?'

He holds open the door for her. 'Please, Miss. I know where you're going. To Crab-apple Cottage, is that right? Mrs Avery, right?'

'Yes – but how did you - ?'

'Easy – not many beautiful young women come here – Oh', as he noticed her quizzical expression, 'I do mean that, Miss, but also Mrs Avery, she happened to mention a few days ago that you were coming to visit her and then she says if you arrived at the station and I was nearby, would I drive you up to the Cottage? just in case you might have forgotten the way - and with luggage -'

'Thank you, Mr Fortune. I love walking, but there'll be time and opportunity for that, I'm sure.'

The distance is greater than I remembered, she was thinking, as they reached a road running up towards a high hill glowing in the setting sun.

'Oh, but those houses are new - when were they built, Mr Fortune?'

'Ten or fifteen years ago, not long after the War, Miss – "the last War" maybe we'll have to say soon if things go on the way they are – Mrs Avery sold that land at the edge of the farm, and you'll see that she sold some fields too, I think she had to – things was hard for all of us then – it's better now – but – they do say another war's just round the corner, don't they – But here's the gate, Miss – No, it's been a pleasure, Miss – No, please, Mrs Avery would never countenance any payment – and she has been very good to me and my family over the years – and especially after my wife died - A lovely lady, Mrs Avery – but you know that – and we all admire her -'

'Thank you so much, Mr Fortune. I hope we'll see each other again – and maybe we can have a cup of tea together? Is the Sunshine Cafe still going? I hope so.'

Three

As the car turned away from her and headed slowly down the hill, Ann heard a shout and turned to see Meg walking fast towards her.

'My dear, my dear, how *lovely*! – after all these years -'

Ann's suitcase was taken from her and deposited near the open gate; then Meg lurched forward, a little breathless, and held her in a tight embrace.

'I never dared to hope this would happen, my dear - that you would come back to us for even a short time! The children are so excited, and even the two grandchildren, none of them can wait to see you, they're coming for tea - But we've got time for a cuppa before they arrive, and a chatter – so much to catch up, isn't there? And please call me Meg, the way you used to, most people still call me that - then I'll feel – oh, that you're really here and that we're back together just like we used to be -'

As they walked up the hill towards the cottage, Ann – regretting that her old habit of racing up the hill towards the big old apple-tree in front of the cottage would no longer be practicable – noticed some changes. The barn looks quite decrepit, yes, but the cottage seems just as sturdy as ever, though it needs repainting. Oh, but - as they came round the barn - the big old apple-tree – no longer exists -

A small black-and-white fox-terrier suddenly appeared and jumped eagerly up at Ann – who loved dogs and immediately squatted to make friends with this one while it licked her hand.

'Oh, that's Skippy, just ignore her. She's a grand-daughter of Ariel, you may remember her, Davey's – Oh – I was going to say "Davey's dog".

Ann, I know I'll be constantly slipping up, I'm just too stupid to control my mouth and keep quiet, and I never could keep secrets anyway. You remember, no self-control, my mother always said that, and she was right - so the sooner we sit down and have our tea and a chat – And anyway we have both moved on – it's going on for twenty years, isn't it? And you look so attractive, my dear, can you really be thirty-nine? Or so? And I'm sixty – *sixty!* - for my sins – getting to be an old woman - But here we are, and welcome, welcome, my dear – welcome again and forever to Crab-apple Cottage.'

Meg, breathing heavily, put down Ann's suitcase and embraced her. Then pushed the door open and they went into warmth: a small fire was burning quietly in the old brick fireplace.

'Make yourself comfortable, my dear. You know your way around this cottage - I'm sure you remember, and nothing's really changed, it's all just as untidy as ever - and quite a bit shabbier no doubt – Oh, the toilet, the washroom you call it, don't you? Yes, you remember where it is - '

Then, at first, as they sat down on opposite sides of the big oak table that dominated the room, both women were suddenly stiff, constrained. The big grandfather-clock in a far corner ticked steadily. Then the kettle on the Aga stove suddenly broke into their silence with its whistle, and Meg jumped up to make tea.

Ann suddenly burst out 'Let's not talk about the War, please, Meg. Everybody seems so obsessed by it - "Is there any chance it won't happen after all?" - "Any chance we won't be dragged in again?" - and so on and so on. Everyone seems incapable of talking about anything else – and we don't know, we can't know, maybe even the Prime Minister doesn't know. Another war! In Canada, when I left, so much worry and talk about it, and on the ship before we were attacked – yes, we were attacked even before war has been declared! And of course it's worse over here – in London, anyway – everybody worrying, talking about it or trying not to talk about it – And even gas-masks! Which are horrible to wear, but they say we may need them, in London anyway – if War does come – but I said Let's not talk about the War, and here I am doing it -' She stopped abruptly, breathless, and reached down to pat Skippy.

'Oh, I agree, my dear. Let's take a vow to not even mention the War. And anyway, I want to know all about *you* and your life in Canada.'

'And I want to know about all of *you*. After so long -'

'They'll be here soon, Jane and Emily and the children, and then you'll be inundated with their lives and activities, I promise. But Will can't come tonight, unfortunately - he has to work this weekend, he told me that last night when I 'phoned to remind him about you coming. He's the Manager of a big shop in London now – Oxford Street. He's done very well, you'll hardly recognize him now, my dear – so mature, not the wild teenager you will remember. How old was he when you last saw him? - sixteen, I think – yes, he was sixteen when Davey – oh, there I go again -'

'Please don't worry, Meg. You can't offend me. *I'm* the one who – I caused so much pain for you all, I know I did. I think I need your forgiveness – all of you -'

'No, no – No. We'll talk later, my dear. All about it. When the children have gone. Before you and I go to bed. And here's your cuppa, at last. Do you take sugar? I can't remember. I hope it's still hot enough. And please help yourself to a scone or two.'

They sat in silence again for a few uncomfortable minutes, sipping their tea.

Then Ann: 'Oh, Meg – I said Let's talk about anything *except* the War, but I must tell you about when our ship was torpedoed – or was it? In the middle of the night - I'll tell you about the whole thing after the others arrive, I don't think I could bear telling it more than once. It was terrible, *horrible* – One passenger died, and they said it was a heart-attack and it was a miracle there weren't more casualties, but – and I think they kept it quiet, they wouldn't even say what it was, whether it was a torpedo – and it wasn't in the news at all, I think – Daddy and Hilda didn't know about it. But I must ask you about the woman I met on the ship who said she knew you, I happened to mention your name when we were chatting, up on the main deck, soon after we left New York – and she said she thought she knew you, she said that you and she had worked together in the last few years to try to prevent another war. She had been a nurse in the War, she said – a V.A.D. like me, but she had also nursed abroad – in France. And now she's a journalist, she said, and also gives lectures to try to motivate people, especially women, to fight against war - and she also wrote a well-known anti-war book, Daddy remembered it – I can't remember the title.'

Meg smiled. 'Yes, I know who you mean, I didn't like her much. I met her after she visited here and then I said I'd help in arranging her talk next time she visits here, and then I joined the P.P.U., the Peace Pledge Union, when it was founded, a short while ago, have you heard of it? Anything to try to stop war - and then I read an article by her, Jane showed it to me in the Library, about how women must work together to prevent war. As I say, I didn't much like her, I thought she was a bit shrill, but -'

Ann: 'Anyway, what was I going to say? She came and sat next to me, I was on the deck, in the sun, and she asked was I American or Canadian and had I served in the War, had I been a Nurse? - said she noticed the way I walked, the way I "held myself" - I still don't see what she meant by that. And then she told me she had been a V.A.D. nurse, and I said that *I* had been a V.A.D. too, though only in England. She had been sent abroad, as I said, to France – and then she said that her cousin – he had been killed too. Oh sorry, Meg - I still start crying whenever – even though it's so long ago -'

Meg reached across the table, patted Ann's hand. 'My dear, I'm so sorry. I can understand how his death – Davey's - We were all so upset too, of course – Will and the girls, as well as me. And now your ship being attacked, and your Father's illness too. You just need time to recover and relax, my dear, I know how it feels – it takes time, doesn't it? Come, have another cuppa, that always helps, I find. And you know, when the girls come, they'll be here soon, you don't need to talk about anything that may hurt you, give you pain – please know that, dear Ann. Just know that we all love you, that you're with family here. And I think I can hear them now. Yes, do you hear?' She stood up, went across to the window and called out 'Coo-ee! You must remember that, Ann? Coo-ee!'

'Oh, yes, I do! I've often remembered it and longed to hear it again. You always shouted it, all of you - coo-ee, coo-ee.' Ann stood up, turned towards the door.

Four

'Jane! Emily!' Meg called loudly. 'We're here, in the kitchen – tea's still hot, come and join us. But where are the children, Emmy?"

'Decided not to bring them – school homework! And also they were playing with friends. But where's - ? Oh there you are.' Emily came into the kitchen and stood still for a moment, staring; then moved aside so Jane could come past her and hug Ann.

The four women stood in a brief silence before Jane said 'Oh Ann, it's so wonderful to see you. Truly! And you look almost the same, hardly any older - but I bet you see a big difference in us, we were just little girls then – twenty or twenty-five years ago, was it? I was only about eight, wasn't I? When we were last together. And Emily was six! Yes, I was eight! Can you believe it?'

Meg: 'Come, you two, let's all sit down, and I'll warm up the tea-pot. Or would you like some wine instead? Yes, yes - let's have some wine, let's celebrate –' And she reached into the back of the kitchen-cupboard. 'Look, it's still here, after all the years! No, I'm joking, Ann – I got it for last Christmas and New Year and then forgot all about it, we don't often drink - Now where's the corkscrew? But this is a very special occasion, isn't it? We'll have to drink out of cups, I don't know where the wine-glasses have got to – Oh come on, now, drink your tea up and hold out your cups -'

'So who or what are we supposed to drink to, Mum, apart from Ann?' Emily asked sharply. 'Preventing the war? The King's good health? The Prime Minister? Absent family and friends? Daddy?'

Ann sat down suddenly, splashing the table with her wine. She forced herself to speak. 'Sorry, I'm so sorry.'

Meg ignored Emily's outburst. 'To Ann and may her visit be very happy.' She sipped her wine, and after a moment so did Jane and Emily, neither of them looking at Ann.

Then Ann stood up, clumsily. 'Do you mind – Can I lie down? – just for a few minutes -'

Meg put down her cup, came round the table to Ann, hugged her and said softly 'Of course, my dear. I'm sorry - I didn't take account of how tired you must be, and with all the worry about your Father. Come and sit beside the fire, maybe we all need to just relax for a few moments.'

When they were all sitting comfortably and Meg had 'given the fire some encouragement', Ann spoke slowly and quietly. 'Sorry to be so disruptive. Please forgive me. I'm feeling better already. So, if you don't mind, let me say my piece now. I've rehearsed it often enough! I tell myself I had some excuse for my bad behaviour twenty years ago, at first anyway: there was Barry and that was a full-time job - more than a full-time job - I can tell you later about Barry, he was my cousin - and why I went back to Canada with him when the War was over – to care for him, and then we got married, but he died last year - we were married for ten years. But – Anyway, I know I was very wrong, after you had all been so kind to me. I was wrong to just go, without even saying goodbye. Of course it had to do with Davey as well as Barry - our relationship –

and his death – all the pain, the unhappiness - I couldn't bear it, I just couldn't bear it. I felt so guilty and – confused – and Daddy had told me about Barry, how he had been badly wounded and blinded at the Battle of Passchendaele and needed nursing.' She turned towards Meg. 'And you were always so good to me, so kind and generous, all of you, I knew I had let you all down, and I just couldn't – I couldn't deal with it, I had to escape, I had to get away. I told myself that Barry needed me – and he did, he did – and he badly wanted to be back in Canada near his family and friends, I knew that. But it was never any justification for – it couldn't be an excuse, nothing could - My behaviour was very wrong, I knew that, but somehow I didn't, I couldn't – So – I need to ask for your forgiveness.'

Meg: 'Oh, Ann, Ann – we were wrong too. We could have – we *should* have understood, or at least guessed – and tried to contact you. It was all so painful and confusing. But now – we're together and -' She reached for Ann's hand.

'Mum's right' Jane said quietly after a moment. 'I remember how hard I found it: Daddy gone, and you gone too, Ann – and all the fun, and the games we played together, all gone, all gone. And the walks. It seemed like everything happy was gone. And Mum, you were gone too, in a way - Mum? – and I remember thinking that Emmy and I just had each other, we even said that, didn't we? – "We just have each other now". And we -'

'- were so sad and unhappy, and angry': Emily. 'Yes, I remember, Jane, of course – it was a painful time, thank goodness we had each other – and it seemed such a long while before any real happiness came back into our lives. Not just for you and me, but also for you, Mum – in some ways, I think you had the worst time of all, because you also had to worry about trying to keep the farm going - and even this cottage too, remember how you told us that we would have to give it up and go and live in Street with Grandad unless something unexpected happened – And how we all prayed together that night, I remember that so well, though we never spoke about it much afterwards – in fact, not until now. And then, because Mr Fortune – and you said to us "Good Fortune has saved us" - remember?'

Meg smiled, sadly. 'Yes. I do remember. Of course. And now here I am still, in this shabby old place. My friends often ask me Isn't it too much for me now, having to walk up and down the hill, and looking after the animals? - And I say that I love the apple-trees, and they think I'm joking. But I do love them – and everything on this farm – the chickens and the sheep and Horace the Horse and Elsie the cow, oh and you too, Skippy,' and she reached down to pat the little fox-terrier, asleep at her feet, 'and this Cottage of course - and the walking's good for me. I also tell my friends how my two daughters always give me such wonderful help – which keeps me going -'

'Oh, Mum – you know what a handful, two handfuls, my kids are. And Roger doesn't help much – well, he can't, his work -'

'Oh, now, Emmy, don't think I'm being sarcastic. I am truly grateful that my two daughters give me so much help, when their lives are so busy – you with the children and Roger, I know how busy you and Roger are - and Jane with the Library and all its responsibilities. Please don't think I'm not grateful for all you two do.'

Emily stood up abruptly. 'Talking of responsibilities, I should be getting home to see about the boys – and their father - they'll be needing their dinner. This was going to be just a short visit. Mum said you might have to rush back to London at any time, Ann. But thank you for not just the tea, and the wine, Mum! - also for our chat. Ann, you won't believe that we haven't had a real talk like this for a good long while, the three of us – so you see, you are doing good already. I hope you'll stay as long as you can. I know you have to be with your Father while he's in hospital, Mum told us about that and we hope he'll be better soon - but whenever you can, please come back and spend more time with us. If Mum gets sick of you, we've got a spare room.'

Jane: 'Yes, Ann - Emily says it for both of us. And I hope you'll look in at the Library? If you have time tomorrow perhaps, or next time you're here. If I'm not at the desk, just knock on the Office door and come in.'

Emily: 'Which reminds me to say that I hope you'll also find time to come to us for a meal – Roger would enjoy meeting you, and the boys are old enough to enjoy games and walks with you, if you would like that. You know, the way you used to play with us, when Jane and I were children.'

Ann smiled. 'Yes, I'd love to do all of those things – thank you. Though please remember, I'm *also* more than twenty years older! I'll phone the hospital tomorrow morning, if that's all right, Meg? and see how my Father is doing.'

Five

'Can I help with the washing-up?' Ann asked as she and Meg returned to the cottage, with Skippy romping ahead, after they had walked with the two younger women down the hill to where Emily's car was parked near the gate.

'No need, Ann. Won't take me a jiffy. And standing at the sink, looking out while I wash up - I always love the twilight' Meg murmured. 'Davey did too – and he loved painting it - Oh there I go again! We must deal with this issue, Ann, don't you think? or we'll never be able to just relax and talk about the past – all the happy times, as well as the unhappy ones. And there *were* happy ones, weren't there? Very happy. And the unhappy ones – well, they say time cures all, don't they? - they can't hurt us now. Oh and that reminds me: I have a project that I hope you'll consider. I'll tell you all about it tomorrow. But I think you need to get to bed – after such a full day -'

'No, actually I feel very – I feel quite tense, I know I wouldn't be able to get to sleep. So please, let's talk a little more – unless *you* are feeling too tired -'

Meg smiled. 'You really haven't changed much, Ann. I was always astonished by your energy – playing with the children, all that rushing about – and then those long walks with Davey. I remember how exhausted I would get, when we first met, Davey and me – all that tramping about the countryside that he loved doing. Sometimes I was grateful that *you* were doing it with him, Ann, when there was so much always to do here, with the children – and just keeping this farm ticking over. Of course Davey always thought of the farm as *my* responsibility – mainly I think because I had grown up here, and of course Dad had left it to me, I was his only child after all. But here I am, talking too much again. And you *must* be tired, Ann – why don't we continue our conversation tomorrow morning when we should both be refreshed and a bit more clear-headed than I feel at this moment?'

'Yes of course, maybe that's best, as you say - I guess I *am* a bit weary – and absorbing the excitement of being here again – the excitement of being with you, and the children. And I was also thinking that I might get a summons back to the hospital - at any moment, I guess. Anyway, you're right, Meg. I'll go off to bed now, and if I oversleep in the morning, please just shake me awake -'

'Oh, I think the cock will wake you up, my dear! But if not, yes, I'll bring you a cuppa to get you going. But let me say again how *lovely* it is to have you! Good-night, Ann, sleep well.'

Six

Ann stirred in the early morning. Had the cock crowed? She got up quickly, washed and dressed. In trousers, shirt and hiking-boots, she felt ready for what she hoped the day would give her: an intense, renewed experience of the nostalgically-remembered English rural life that she'd tasted before the Great War, and even for a while *during* its first two years. So long ago – but now it's beginning to seem like yesterday -

A knock at the door, and Meg came in, carrying a tray with tea, boiled egg, an apple, and sandwiches. 'Oh, you're up already, Ann. I hope you slept well?'

'Oh, yes – the bed's very comfortable, but I could have slept on a board I was so tired – and now I feel so refreshed. I didn't even hear the cock crowing. Can I take my breakfast and sit in one of those chairs just outside the front door?'

'Yes, of course, my dear.' Meg turned and started towards the stairs. 'And then we can feed the chicks and animals before we have our big talk – which I'm looking forward to, at least as much as you. It's a lovely day! And the girls are coming this afternoon, did I mention that? - bringing Emily's children, as they often do on a Sunday - the boys love coming here. But this time it's special – so I hope you won't get a summons back to London before then.'

'I hope not too – and also, that would indicate that Daddy's all right – I mean if there's no call. The nurses promised me they'd call if there was any need. And actually he said – Daddy – he can still talk, but they try to keep him calm so he doesn't tire himself – he said not to drop everything all the time to be with him.'

'Well, I'll go and feed Elsie, that's our old cow, she doesn't give much milk now but she's a lovable old girl - and also there are the sheep, and Horace the old horse, both boys love to ride him . You eat your breakfast, I hope it's enough for you. I don't eat much now and I'm likely to under-estimate your needs, so just shout. And I should mention, too, that I'm a vegetarian now.'

'Me too! - almost. Maybe you'll inspire me to make the final effort.'

The morning was calm and clear. As she ate, Ann was aware of being at ease for the first time in several months – in fact, since, well, 'since before Barry's death', she told herself. And she became aware of birdsong, too, in the nearby apple-trees – and a few sparrows had appeared, nearby, clearly hoping for remnants of the toast she was eating.

Soon Meg was back, breathing quite heavily. 'Finished? Had enough? Well, come and be introduced to the animals, and you can help me feed the chickens – I've done the sheep - and then we'll wash-up and sit down and talk about sealing-wax and kings and other things, is that how that quotation goes? And then I thought you'd like to have a walk up to the Hut before lunch? Yes?'

'You're so good to me, Meg.'

'Oh, don't worry, you'll find yourself running the whole farm, what's left of it, if you talk like that.'

Soon, back at the Cottage, they were sitting companionably in two old armchairs - 'They ought to be turfed and replaced,' Meg said 'but they're just too darn comfortable to get rid of. The girls tell me they're embarrassingly ugly and dirty, and probably full of obscure diseases - but I just pretend I'm deaf and blind. And now - who's going to go first? Seems we both have things we want to say. Well, you tell me, in just a few words, what - Your letter told me some things, but you said yourself there was so much more. I think you said you are still a nurse?'

'Yes. But not in a hospital any more, not for quite a while – I nurse in a Home, an Old People's Home, where Barry was for over ten years – before he died, several months ago – almost a year ago. He was severely wounded, I think I told you that, at Passchendaele – so many Canadian soldiers were - and he was blind. I was nursing him, near the end of the war, and he -'

'You fell in love with him?'

'No. No, I couldn't. He was my cousin. And anyway I was -'

'Oh, my dear, my dear. Don't be afraid to say it. I know. You were in love with Davey, weren't you? Lots of us were. He was - very lovable. Now, you see, you'll have me crying any moment. But it was his talent that also attracted so many people. Did you know there was a special retrospective showing of his war paintings and sketches in London? Maybe it's still on, I think I have the programme somewhere, I'll look for it – they invited me and the children to its Opening. Last Spring. And he wrote articles about the countryside, and composed music too – did you know? He had such a lovely voice, he had been a choirboy – and sang in his college chapel at Cambridge - before I met him of course. Sometimes I could persuade him to sing, and I would accompany him on the old piano - it's gone now, it was so out of tune and anyway I couldn't bear to play it, or listen to it, afterwards. And he even wrote poetry, about the glories of Nature – and how the War attacked and almost destroyed Nature. I haven't shown it to anyone. He asked me not to. But maybe I'll show you one or two of his earlier poems later, Jane thinks they are very good, the ones she's seen. He had so many talents, Davey! But I'm just rambling, my dear – again - You've opened the tap and out it's all flowing, all my memories, all that I haven't been able to talk about, or even think about, for so long – But now -'

'Actually I think I need to – exercise, walk. Is that all right? Do you mind? You said his Hut – the garden-house?'

'But first, Ann – What's the time, can you see the clock? Is it eleven o'clock? Yes?'

'Yes. Actually ten minutes *after* eleven.' Ann was puzzled.

'Good. Then I'll switch on the wireless. I listened to the BBC news early this morning, and they said there would be an important Announcement by the Prime Minister, about the German response to our Government's ultimatum that they must leave Poland – now they must agree to leave by eleven o'clock this morning. Our reception here's not so good but -'

And at eleven-fifteen, they heard the trembling voice of Neville Chamberlain, Prime Minister, announcing that, as no response had been received from the German Government by the communicated time, Great Britain was now at war.

The two women looked at each other in silence. What was there to say? For so many months, even years, war with Germany had seemed ever more likely.

After a few minutes, Ann said 'Well, I'm glad I brought my gas-mask with me – we were told at the hospital that we should always have our gas-masks with us, wherever we go – and of course everyone must be aware already of air-raid shelters, barrage-balloons, the Black-out, and crowds of children being evacuated from London in trains and buses. So now it's all official. War has been declared.'

Meg sighed. 'Yes. No surprise to any of us. But now our fear will spread and deepen, I suppose.' She stood up to switch off the wireless, then turned to Ann. 'We mustn't let ourselves get depressed, must we? So let's go on as we intended with the day – and it's another beautiful sunny day! So no more of my chattering. I've got a few things to do now, in the Cottage, Ann, but you go on up to Davey's Hut, that's what he called it, as you'll remember. It's almost how it was, in the old days - like this Cottage – and I've put a few of his paintings out for you to see – ones they didn't want for the exhibition because they're landscapes, not war-paintings - you'll recognise some of the subjects, I'm sure - countryside you'll remember from your walks – so I put them there, in the Hut, where he painted them. Well, as I say, the organisers of the exhibition didn't want them - just the sketches he did at the Front, and the paintings, of trenches and explosions and wounded soldiers and so on, that he did from his sketches or from his memory during his leave. He was killed, well you know this, don't you? - in 1918, the Battle of Passchendaele, like your cousin – Well, your cousin was wounded, and blinded you said, but Davey – they said it was a direct hit, and – there was almost nothing left of him, apparently, so at least one could hope he didn't suffer – it was not long after he got back to the Front – Oh, listen to me, gabbling on, Ann – Go on up to his hut now, I've got things to do in the kitchen – like making their favourite what-*you*-call cookies, for the children -'

Seven

Led excitedly by Skippy - 'Just as if you know where I must go' Ann thought – she reached the Hut perched on top of the steep hill behind the Cottage, and leaned for a few moments against the big old oak tree beside it to catch her breath. The day was sharp and clear, with a few clouds slowly drifting by; and the view – yes, just as she remembered it – so verdant - 'radiant', she remembered saying to Davey when they first climbed up to the Hut. 'Look around' he had commanded in a satirical tone, 'earth hath not anything to show more fair. South, you can almost see the ocean. West, Wales. North, is that Scotland I see glimmering in the distance? And East – oh, the two Clumps, look, look at them, noble protuberances both, but smaller than our one, their Big Brother, our noble dominating Cloud Clump -' and he had flung his arms wide, 'our Heavenly Heap, on which, even now, we stand and marvel at the endless beauty of Nature. Stop me, or I'll be quoting more poetry!'

She smiled as she remembered his expansive gesture, his enthusiasm;

then turned to the door and pushed it open. Yes, the Hut *does* smell rather damp, musty.

Her canine companion showed no interest in following her into the Hut, and hurtled away, yapping. She went in, slowly.

Several canvases were set against the far wall, behind Davey's old wooden chair. Apart from the canvases and chair, the Hut was empty. And clearly it could not last much longer – the wooden walls were badly discoloured where water had leaked in through the roof, which was rotting. And what about mould? In fact, Ann thought, the survival of the Hut to this point was quite surprising – so many years after the death of the man who had constructed it. Almost the first thing he had said to her when they left Street Station to walk to the Farm, Ann recalled, was 'You must see my Hut, we'll go up there after we've had tea – Come on! Let's march!' Always so eager!

And that had happened so soon after they first met. She had taken the train out of London, intending to spend the day at Brighton, near the sea. And was alone in a second-class compartment, until, just as the journey began, he had suddenly appeared and thrown himself down beside her, already talking, 'Hullo, I'm Davey'. Later she would see how shy and even withdrawn he often was, how he could be embarrassingly silent with strangers, and even with family and old friends - even with her sometimes. So then, why had he approached her so confidently on that first occasion - so friendly and chatty? Because he had noticed that she was obviously dressed to go walking - pants and boots? No, that wasn't likely. Or was it entirely fortuitous, was he simply in one of his unpredictable positive moods? When she had asked him once, later, about that first encounter, he had only smiled mischievously and said 'Oh, you looked so available.'

By the time the train reached Street, they were in enthusiastic conversation (what about? She couldn't remember, but surely very much about the country-walks that he knew so well, especially around Edge. 'And you must meet my wife Margaret and my three children, you must have lunch with us, and I'll show you some walks and views that you'll never forget, the best in all England!') Yes, such an enthusiast! I'm remembering that day more vividly now than I ever did before. And what a glorious, unforgettable day it was! Truly, I think I fell in love with him then – Yes, by the time he walked with me to Street that evening, so I could catch the train back to London, I was already in love with him. Oh, what a glorious day it was! Of *course* I wanted to go back there, to

Crab-apple Farm – I couldn't wait to be with him again, walking along those country paths, and in the afternoon playing games with him and Will and the two little girls – and then Meg calling us in for tea - 'Cooee! Cooee!'

Eight

'So what do you think of them?' Meg asked. 'I'm so glad I kept them – they aren't connected with the War, anyway. As I said, they only wanted war-scenes, for the Exposition I mean, especially the sketches Davey did while he was at the Front, and the paintings he did from them, or from his memory, when he was home on leave – It was such a happy time, that leave – he spent all of it here, with us. And the children too, they were so happy. He would come up here early in the morning and just paint and paint – all those war scenes, from his notebook sketches, and from his memories, as I said - And I had to go into Reading and buy him more and more canvases - we couldn't afford it, but he just had to have them, I knew that, so I borrowed money from an uncle in Oxford – And Davey worked and worked up here all morning, but the children would come up in the afternoons, and make him come down the hill and join them for games and walks, Will especially – Oh, you'd have loved those times - No, sorry, I shouldn't say that, my dear – and we didn't know that you were nursing your cousin, and so many other poor wounded young men. If only we'd known! - That woman I mentioned, the one you met on the boat, who had been a V.A.D. nurse like you, I heard her speak, in Street Library, about the dreadful suffering of wounded soldiers she had nursed, especially the ones who were gassed. And when Davey – when the telegram came, saying that he had been killed, it was terrible, terrible, we cried and cried, me and the girls - but at least he wasn't gassed, he didn't go on suffering and suffering, we were grateful for that, to know it had been sudden, a shell that exploded in his trench, that's what they said - several other men were killed. But I've told you that, haven't I? Oh, Ann, I'm so sorry, gabbling on and on like this, why am I doing it? Now, so many years later - Well, we both know about the horrors of that war, you more than me because you actually nursed some of those poor men. Sorry, I'll stop -'

And Meg steadied herself against the doorway, breathing heavily. Ann was standing very still, gazing at the paintings. One of them was of the old apple-tree in blossom, and beside it a figure she had immediately recognised as herself. Meg followed her gaze. 'Yes, my dear, I know what you're thinking, and I thought that too. It's you. And you must have it. He would have wanted that.'

Ann turned, and stepped impulsively towards Meg. They embraced.

Meg: 'And now let's go down for lunch. I'm sure you must be hungry. And remember, we're going to have that conversation. Though I think we've cleared the air already, haven't we? Oh, and I must remember to tell you that Will has telephoned. He apologised for not being able to come yesterday – I said I'd give you his telephone-number, so you and he can meet in London sometime soon. And I told him about your Father. Oh and that reminds me – I wanted to talk to you about that other situation – more complicated, so I'll save it for over lunch. So come, let's go down. And if you'll bring that painting of you and the apple-tree, I'll pack it for you to take back to London tomorrow.'

Meg called Skippy as they set off, and he preceded them eagerly - a small procession down the track to the cottage.

Nine

But Ann was summoned back to London that afternoon – her father was calling out for her, the nurse said. 'Don't rush, just come as soon as you can, dearie.' Before the 'phone rang, though, she and Meg had lunched and conversed lightly, and then Emily had arrived with her children and husband.

Ann liked Roger immediately. Some might find him a bit rough, she thought, but he seemed downright, honest, and was very good with his two boys. He was the only son of a prominent local builder who had bought the lower part of Meg's property in the 1920s and built the houses on it. Roger had inherited his father's business, and his prominent role in the community.

The three of them, Roger and his two small sons, ran about kicking a soccer ball he'd brought; then they played French Cricket while the three women enjoyed their decorous tea nearby, watching and chatting quietly at a picnic-table beside the lawn; and then Ann was pressed to join the boys, now shrieking enjoyment as they kicked the ball to each other.

'A bit different from the games we played in the past' Ann had commented, 'but then we were girls of course – no rough play, and no cheating allowed! Will was usually off playing with the local lads anyway, and Davey didn't always join us: sometimes he retired to his painting, didn't he? But I mustn't miss that train. 5:30, did you say?'

Emily: 'Yes, so you'll have to win your game quickly. Roger will drive you to the station.'

Meg: 'Oh, I hope Fortune doesn't see that – he told me I must tell him when you need to get to the station. But Ann, I'm looking forward to our little jaunt next Sunday, assuming your Father stays well enough for you to come. I'll tell Martha. She will be so pleased that you can be with us.'

Ann joined Roger and the boys for a final kick-about, then hurried indoors to repack her suitcase, which Roger then insisted on carrying down to his vehicle.

The train was quite full, but Ann found a seat quickly. She felt tired, glad to close her eyes and relax. Nobody tried to converse with her - English reticence has its occasional virtue, she told herself.

Ten

In London, she hurried straight to the Hospital by Underground and bus, and was relieved to find her Father in a better state than she had feared; in fact, he was sitting up in his bed and, she was told by a nurse, had even smiled when she told him a joke.

Less welcome was the presence of his second wife, Hilda, who had always shown a cold negativity, even hostility, towards Ann - and had made it clear that Ann's presence, even if valued by her Father, was inconsequential at best. 'Maybe she thought you're after his money' Meg had commented with a smile.

With Hilda was her elderly mother, slumped in the other arm-chair and fast asleep. There were no other chairs. So, rather than continue standing at a distance, Ann perched on the edge of her Father's bed. 'It's so good to see you sitting up, Daddy.' She took his nearest hand and lifted it to her lips while Hilda stiffened in disapproval.

He winked at Ann - or she thought he did – a conspiratorial gambit dating back to whenever his first wife, Ann's Mother, who had died during the Measles Epidemic after the end of the First World War, voiced criticism of him - as she had done frequently when the marriage began to fracture.

Now, to her surprise, Ann found herself suddenly close to tears. She kissed his hand again. What should she talk to him about? It was almost a relief when a nurse came to her and whispered 'There's someone who would like to speak to you. Can you come away for a few minutes?'

Leaning close to her Father, she said quietly 'Daddy, I have to go away but I'll be back in a few minutes.' Then she smiled briefly at her stepmother and followed the nurse out of the room.

Standing at the nurses' desk was – No, no – No -

She hesitated, then went to him, as he turned towards her. Yes, it's *Will*. It's Will. But it could, it really could – it could almost be Davey. Before he grew his beard. But Will's broader, thicker-set. With dark wiry hair, blue eyes.

He took her hand in silence.

Yes, but Davey never wore a suit, she was thinking. Never looked so smart.

'Hullo, Ann' he said quietly. A soft deep voice, like Davey's – but softer, deeper.

And it came to her suddenly that Meg and Jane and Emily had said very little – hardly anything, in fact - about Will. Was there a rift? She responded to him now, matching his calm tone. 'Hi, Will. Lovely to see you. After so long. I'm so -'

'No' he said. 'No apologies, no explanations.'

She smiled. 'But how do you know what I was going to say?'

'Because I'm clairvoyant, Ann. Oh, all right, it's because Mum said that in your letter you were so apologetic about what happened twenty years ago. But we've all moved on, Ann. Or should have. No point in going over the old ground. We can talk a bit more about that if you want to, later - but mostly I hope we can talk about other things, cheerful things. If you can come to dinner with me – that's what I'm hoping – why I'm here now, actually. At a restaurant nearby. Why don't you go back to your Father now – Mum told me about that, his heart-attack – and I'll wait here. There's a comfortable couch I can see, along the passage. All right?'

'All right. I'll try not to be too long.' And she went back to her Father.

Hilda stirred and announced suddenly 'Mummy is very tired, it's past her bedtime, and she isn't well, in fact she's not any better than Arthur really, it's hard for her coming here but I can't leave her on her own. We may not be able to come again for a few days – Mummy really isn't up to it, I'm afraid.'

After Hilda and her mother had gone, Ann sat, with some relief, in one of the vacated chairs, which she drew up close to the bed. But her Father was deeply asleep now, and snoring softly.

When a nurse bustled in, Ann mentioned that she would have to leave soon, if it was all right to do so? 'Yes, yes, dearie, you've got your life to live too. Just check at the desk to make sure we have your telephone number, in case we need to contact you urgently. But he's looking so much better now, don't you think? More settled. Probably because you have been with him again. He relaxes when you're with him. I'll get the bed flat so he can sleep properly. See you tomorrow morning.'

Ann smiled her thanks and went along the passage.

Will stood up when he saw her coming. They looked at each other awkwardly, in silence, before he said 'The restaurant's nearby, walking distance. Italian. All right? I suppose you're getting used to the Black-out? Some people are already frightened to go out at night now.'

'Oh, I'm just careful not to go far at night – and the walks between the hospital and my little hotel, and the Underground, are short and easy.'

The proprietor clearly knew Will and led them to a secluded table.

When they had ordered, Will leaned forward. He spoke softly but fiercely. 'Why are you here? Or rather, why did you write to Mum, why do you want to connect with us again, after so long? Don't you think you did enough damage? And then you just disappeared, no word, no message, how do you think we felt? And Mum struggling with her grief. How could you be so cruel?'

Ann sat in silence, shocked by his sudden intensity. Then said hesitantly 'My Father -'

'Oh, I know about his heart-attack, etcetera etcetera, Mum told me - that's why I was at the hospital, of course - waiting for you. And Mum wanted me to be with them earlier, to welcome you, that's what she said. To *welcome* you! Have you no idea what you did, how we felt?'

'But – I'm sorry, sorry, but -'

'Sorry! Sorry! Do you think that's enough - just to say sorry, sorry – and Dad – *my* Father, remember *him*? the one who was slaughtered in that little war a few years ago -'

Ann stood up to leave. But a waiter was approaching with an opened bottle of wine, so she sat down again, shakily. No, I *will not cry*, she ordered herself. But what has happened, why is he suddenly so different? Attacking me like that. She turned her face away. I feel sick. I want to leave, I want to go away, far away. But then she turned back and looked across the table into his eyes.

They sat in silence. He tasted the wine and nodded acceptance to the waiter, who went.

Then he cleared his throat. 'I suppose you think – Oh, hell, so what do we do now? – But I'm not going to apologise – it needed to be said, I needed to say it – and now I've said it -'

'Yes, you have, you really have.' But, to her own surprise, she felt relief – relief from the tension that had invaded her since she received the message, in Toronto, that her Father was in hospital after a heart-attack, and had been calling for her. And she had had to make urgent arrangements and hope to get a quick boat passage (she had always hated air-travel, the confinement, the noise). But then her Father had been sent home, for a few months before a second heart-attack. And after that -

'Yes, you have' she said again. 'And so what do we do now?'

Will cleared his throat again. Then he said 'What we do is drink to the future – may this war be an improvement on the last' and he smiled slightly. 'Come on, that's a good wish, isn't it? Drink to the future – And I see our soup is about to arrive – so drink, Ann, that's right. And I'll also drink to your father, may he recover quickly - and even to *you*, I drink to you, Ann, may your visit be – what? What do you want? - happy? A happy visit. Let's drink to that. A happy visit!'

'For all of us' Ann added.

They clicked glasses and drank, smiling wryly at each other.

Then they chatted, with many short silences, about the War and the inconveniences of the Black-out and gas-masks etcetera - avoiding as much as possible any references to their common past. And, she realised later, any references to his mother and sisters, apart from a few generalities.

As soon as the meal was over, he said 'But you must be very tired. I'll see you to your hotel. We can get together again and talk a bit about the past, if you like? Now that we're beginning to know each other again. I've got lots to say. How about you?'

'Yes' she said. 'I would like.'

Back in her small hotel-room half-an-hour later, Ann realised that she was unexpectedly happy and at ease for the first time since she had received news of her Father's first heart-attack, and, a day after that, had decided she must contact Meg – decided reluctantly, she remembered, and in the discomfort of a renewed sense of guilt.

But now she wondered whether, in the sad emptiness after Barry's death, intense memories of her time in England had returned to pacify her, and whether her father's illness had in fact been the main cause of her decision to travel back to England. 'To return and face the music' she said aloud to the mirror, as she washed her face and cleaned her teeth, before climbing into bed and falling immediately into a deep sleep.

Eleven

A few weekends later, at Meg's suggestion they met in Street at the Sunshine Cafe, close to the Station, and had a late breakfast together.

The day was vigorous – sunny with a sharp breeze from the West. 'You can smell the sea' Ann enthused. 'Oh, how I long to go to the coast! "To the lonely sea and the sky -"' and she remembered how meeting Davey had thwarted her the first time she had wished that, so many years ago, but also how several of their subsequent long walks had led them to the sea, how they had roamed beaches collecting shells for Jane and Emily, how they had once hired a small boat and frolicked round the harbour in it, how they – But then Meg's smiling face came into focus, and she thought But it never even occurred to me that, while we two roamed the countryside and enjoyed ourselves, Meg was keeping the family together and the farm in good order – doing what had to be done - Oh, we were selfish, weren't we, Davey and I -? Well, *I* was. And she wondered briefly if Davey had ever -

Meg: 'A penny for your thoughts, my dear – no, I'd have to pay more now, wouldn't I? All that worry about the Economy, and the Depression, the Dirty Thirties as someone said – and so many workers and their families suffering, especially in the North – the miners, farmers – it's a worrying time, even without all the concern now about war. Some people say that Hitler is even more determined to attack us now, and *will* attack us just as soon as the Germans have the rest of Europe under their control. And all the Prime Minister's efforts to dissuade the Germans were useless, those people say - So now any of your thoughts would be worth more than a penny, wouldn't they, Ann! But just listen to me going on and on, my dear! And we have so many things to think about, and talk about, haven't we? By the way, you can leave your knapsack here, Fortune will keep it safe.'

Ann: 'Sorry, Meg. I'm being rude again. Now I'm back here, with you, with your family, and also with Daddy, and renewing so many vivid memories from the past - sorry, my mind jumps all over the place. I never had much self-control – you used to say that, didn't you, and you also say that I haven't changed much-'

'Yes, but I was wrong, I think you *have* changed, my dear. In some important ways. So let's -'

'For the better? No, I don't think so. And unlike you, dear Meg, I do need to change. And I *will* change, and make up for the past, or die trying to. And I haven't told you yet about meeting Will last Sunday night, though maybe *he* has?'

Meg smiled and sipped her tea. 'Oh, Ann. Time for that later and I have things to tell *you*. Anyway, let's do some planning for today and tomorrow, hoping that you won't be summoned back to London earlier than tomorrow afternoon.' She was looking hard over Ann's right shoulder. 'And in a few minutes, Martha will arrive – Oh, no time now for talking and planning. Here she is!'

Ann turned to look over her shoulder. The white-haired woman walking rapidly towards them was slim and smiling, in a long black skirt. Meg stood up and they embraced.

Ann also stood up, just in time for a long tight hug, Martha crowing 'But we already know each, Ann, don't we, because our dear mutual friend Meg has told us all about each other – but also we know we're nicer than she says we are, aren't we? And you're a nurse, and were a V.A.D. in the War, weren't you? The last war. Lots to talk about! So, are we going to catch that bus, Meg? He'll be waiting for us – I wouldn't want him to think we aren't coming, and get agitated. I told him very specifically that we'd go for a walk before lunch, and I know he'll be waiting impatiently – he loves a taste of the countryside, as you know, Meg.'

Ann was puzzled and Meg, noticing this, said 'Sorry, Ann - somehow I never got into telling you all about it, we always seem to have had so much else to talk about – and so little time - but Martha and I will tell you all you need to know in the bus – about where we're going and why. And it's almost time for it, so let's go across to the bus-stop. You can leave your knapsack here – I'll tell them we'll be back for it later.'

It was difficult to talk in the bus, as it was crowded with evacuated children and their guardians, and noisy with their chatter about local issues and the War. After about half-an-hour, Martha leaned across to say loudly 'Next stop. Just follow me.'

Twelve

The building was very big and shabby, with Ionic pillars guarding its main entrance – a Victorian remnant, Ann thought.

The three women climbed a dozen grimy steps and Martha pressed a large bell twice. After a short wait, an elderly woman in a faded blue habit opened the door just wide enough for them to follow her while she announced over her shoulder 'Good morning, I'm Sister Helen,' and then, when they reached a large desk, 'Have any of you visited before?"

'Yes, I have' Martha responded. 'To see Peter Arnold. I hope he is -'

'Oh yes, I remember you. Yes. You have visited him a few times.' Sister Helen indicated a ledger: 'Please sign here, all of you. I'm not sure that Mr Arnold will be in a good state to see you all at once. If he is, we request that you all remain in the Garden, near the side door, and immediately inform us if he becomes unwell or agitated. And his Minder will be nearby. Is that understood?'

'Yes, Sister. Thank you.'

While they waited, Martha told Meg and Ann, in a low voice, that she had visited Peter Arnold first at the request of his mother, a very elderly lady in the local old people's home. 'He was badly wounded in the Second Battle of Ypres - "Wipers" as they called it, the lads who fought in that terrible battle. Maybe you know that the Germans used poison-gas, quite illegally, in that battle. Peter was one of the casualties – lucky to have survived at all, apparently, and his Mother told me that his mental state even before the War had been precarious – he had wanted to be an artist, she told me, but – Anyway, it seems that he met your husband, Meg, as I told you - when they both walked the Downs and areas near here before the First War. His Mother said they would sleep under hedges if the weather allowed it, and that's how they came to know each other. And when I mentioned your husband's name last time I was here, he immediately looked hard at me and whispered "I knew him – Davey was my friend" and, as I told you, when I asked if he would like to meet you, he just closed his eyes and took my hand and held it – so I knew that Yes, he would – and last time, when you couldn't come, Meg, he was clearly very disappointed, and when I mentioned it was because *you* were here, Ann, from Canada, he gripped my hand very tight and whispered "Her too, I knew her, she was beautiful – and kind -". Did you bring those maps you mentioned, Meg? I'm sure he will be very interested in them.

You can see why I'm so grateful to you both for coming. But if you think it might upset you -'

Meg looked at Ann, queryingly. 'Do you have any memory of having met him?'

'Oh, yes,' Ann replied quietly, 'I remember him as one of Davey's acquaintances – meeting him along a path or in a pub, by chance. I always felt sorry for him, he seemed so – alone, so - innocent – But I wonder if he'll – how he'll react -'

'Well, we'll know soon enough' whispered Martha. 'Here comes Sister Helen. And with his nurse. We can talk more about him later and decide if we can help any further.'

The nurse was brusque and to the point. 'Hullo. Thank you for your concern about Peter. Of course I recall your previous visits, Miss Blair, and that they had a positive effect. But remember that he can be very unpredictable. If he shows any sign of panic or confusion or anger, please call me or his Minder immediately – we will be nearby. I hope your visit goes well. If you wait outside in the garden, his Minder will escort him to you. After the visit, I would like to talk to you before you leave.'

The Garden was small but well cared-for, and there were several chairs placed in casual circles. Meg and Martha sat down, and chatted quietly. Ann looked round the garden, then stood nearby.

In a short while, Peter arrived, with the Minder – a plump smiling middle-aged lady – at his side. He looked warily at the three women, then closed his eyes and began to moan quietly. The Minder whispered encouragement to him, then withdrew to a chair in the shade of the oak tree. Martha went to him, saying cheerfully 'Peter, how lovely to see you again! And I've brought two friends to meet you, Meg and Ann. And Meg has something I know you're going to find interesting, you probably remember them, David will have shown them to you – they are some of the maps he made of his walks and you'll be able to look at them, he loved drawing maps, and maybe you'll remember some of the walks too. So come over and sit near me.'

Ann watched as Martha took Peter's hand and led him to where Meg was unfolding and laying out, on a picnic-table, a carefully-inked National Survey map showing a path running to the Two Clumps, and then around them back towards Street. Peter was immediately interested, and whimpered with apparent pleasure, bouncing slightly in his chair. With her right forefinger, Meg ostentatiously traced the route from, and back to, Crab-apple Farm, while Martha chattered enthusiastically about the path, the trees, the river, the Clumps. Until suddenly a whimper sharpened into a shout, and Peter jumped up from his chair and ran gesticulating towards Ann, who flinched away from him and smiled but didn't say anything.

The Minder came across to them, led Peter back to his chair, and said quietly to Ann 'Don't worry, my love, he's just frisky today and wanting to be friendly – probably now getting hungry too. But he was clearly interested, Miss Blair, wasn't he?'

Then Peter started to wail, more and more loudly until the Minder pulled up a chair and sat beside him. She said quietly to Martha 'I'm afraid that's it for this visit, Miss Blair. But he'll remember those maps and next time – I should say also that I think he's not at his best with more than one visitor – maybe somehow it confuses him, or makes him remember being wounded and helpless in hospital.'

As they were walking back to the bus-stop, Martha said to Ann 'Thank you for coming, my dear. If you can come again, maybe on your own or with Meg, you'd see how much he loves a visit. This time, towards the end, his obsessive memories of the war and his long hospital stays seemed to be hurting him – did you notice how he was almost beginning to scream at his Minder before she managed to calm him down? But he was looking at you, Ann, often, and I think that was significant.'

Thirteen

'So you didn't realise, did you?'

They were back in the cafe, drinking cups of tepid tea, essentially killing time until Martha needed to cross to the station to catch her train.

Meg: 'Realise what?'

'I'm disappointed in both of you, I must say. Or should I be relieved?' Martha smiled, wryly. 'That he's my brother – half-brother actually – did you really not notice or guess? The woman I mentioned, in the Old People's Home, is his mother and my stepmother. I try to visit him regularly now, but it's not easy, as you can see. Poor Peter! He didn't deserve so much suffering. And for so long – it must be about twenty-five years. Twenty-five years of pain and confusion! I tried to say that to the family but they – Oh, anyway, life can be very cruel, can't it? But my train will be arriving soon and I want to say to you both, but especially to you, Ann, that he was clearly moved and – responsive to you, and so

– if you can manage to come and visit him, on your own, I know he'll be responsive and it could make a big difference, possibly. So I'll telephone tomorrow and speak again to that Sister Helen, I know they'll be only too pleased if you can find the time – Oh, and I'd better get across to the station, the train will be here any moment. It was lovely to meet you, Ann, and to see you both. Don't come across – finish your tea at leisure. Thank you so much – for accompanying me to visit Peter - and for the tea.' She stood up, checked for her ticket in her bag, smiled at them, and walked swiftly across the road.

'Lovely to see you!' Meg called after her, and then said to Ann softly 'Well. She's very intense, don't you think? I don't know why she concealed her relationship at first -'

Ann could think of nothing appropriate to say, except 'That makes two of us. Isn't that – well, an amazing coincidence?'

'Two of you? I don't see -'

'Two of us who have, or in my case *had*, close relatives badly wounded in the War who we felt we had to help afterwards – oh, I'm just chattering, Meg. Take no notice.'

They sat in silence for a few moments.

Then Meg: 'Don't forget your knapsack, now! Oh, I must tell you about tonight, Ann. You'll be thinking I tell you nothing and just push you around. It's just that increasingly life moves too fast for me. I'm just a poor feeble creature trying to catch up with herself.' She smiled sardonically. 'But, Ann – you remember we talked about that pacifist woman you met on the boat? She is still giving speeches urging all women to work for peace – even now, after War has been declared, and maybe any moment bombs will start falling on us - and the local authority, and lots of ordinary people, are building more bomb-shelters, and we've all been told to clear out our cellars in case we need to spend nights in them - if things suddenly get really bad – and the Black-out and rationing – and of course there's even greater urgency, *you* will know, in London? And searchlights and those ugly Blimp-things overhead? But what was I saying? Yes, that she's coming to talk to us in the parish hall tonight, Jane's been asked to chair the meeting – and there may be a chance for you to have a few words with her before she goes back to London, apparently she said she couldn't think of staying overnight this time. So we should get back to the Cottage soon, I have some pies to put in the oven. And Fortune said he'll drive us home now, I just have to 'phone him – Jane will pick us up tonight and also drive us home afterwards. Won't be a moment.' She got up and went to the counter to telephone Mr Fortune, leaving Ann to try to absorb the day's unexpected intensities.

Soon, the taxi arrived and Ann was responding to deferential questions from Mr Fortune: he was clearly troubled about the political situation. Did Ann know anything about what was happening at Westminster? Were preparations for a possible Nazi Invasion intensifying, was the Prime Minister being supported in Parliament? And what had Ann heard about Dominion and American support for the British Government? She satisfied his urgent curiosity as best she could, but knew she fell short.

'I'm sorry I don't know more, Mr Fortune. I've been spending most of my time with my Father, in the hospital, I'm afraid. Everyone's very worried, of course, and waiting and hoping and trying not to think or talk too much about it – you know, "careless talk costs lives" - and clearing out their cellars and building bomb-shelters – and of course there's the Black-out - Oh, if only – but I guess we still have to wait and see -'

'Yes, thank you, Miss.' As always, too deferential, Ann was thinking. Oh, that ugly destructive English class-system!

As they walked up towards the Cottage, she said 'I'll feed the hens and animals.'

'Oh, thank you, my dear. I warned you, didn't I, that you'll soon be responsible for running the whole farm, what's left of it, I mean?'

'But it's a pleasure. It really is, Meg.'

'It's my good fortune, dear Ann, that you're so kind and helpful. I hope we might be able to talk briefly, at supper - or later, if you're not too tired - about some of the things on my mind. No, I won't say anything now - we have too much to do. But I do need your opinions and advice. - Oh, and about Christmas – you know how we'd love you to come then, but I'm sure you'll want to spend that day with your Father – and maybe you couldn't be away from the Hospital, anyway?'

'Yes, so many nurses want to be at home with their families. But thank you – and of course I'll be thinking of you all and hoping you're having a great time!'

Fourteen

Meg and Ann arrived at the Church Hall, at 6:30, an hour before the Speaker was due – she was to be met at the Station by the Vicar's wife, who knew her, and who was also in charge of Refreshments.

'I hope we have a reasonable turn-out' the Vicar said. 'I fear that many in the congregation think that, now the War has officially begun, even though we have not been attacked by the Nazis – or not *yet* – so they think that there is now no point in working for peace, and that we should all concentrate on preparations for attack or even invasion. I fear that many do not even pray, and ask God to save us from our sinful selves.'

Jane and Meg prepared the refreshments-table and boiled water for the tea. Ann helped the Vicar with the Speaker's table and chairs. Then they sat down to await the Speaker's arrival. Twenty minutes before the advertised time, a few people arrived, and sat quietly chatting. And finally, just as Ann was thinking that the meeting might be aborted, the Speaker appeared, with a tall thin white-haired man she introduced as her husband. They were accompanied by the Vicar's wife. Ann came forward hesitantly.

'Oh, Jane, how good to see you again, and thank you for arranging this occasion' the Speaker said loudly, grasping Jane's hand.

'I'm not sure how many -' Jane began hesitantly.

'Oh, however many, we must spread the word, mustn't we? Many people are worried and distressed, we must encourage them as much as possible. Who knows what we might have to suffer if our political leaders can't be sensible and understand that war is completely outmoded now – we of the War Generation, we who fought the War to End Wars, we know that, don't we?"

Then she reached across to Ann and took her hand. "You and I know each other, don't we? Yes, I remember – we met on the high seas and you admitted to having been a nurse, like me, in the First War. I'm so glad you are here. I hope there'll be a few moments for us to talk afterwards, before Desmond and I have to catch the train back to London.'

She was introduced efficiently by Jane, quietening the small crowd of locals. And the talk began.

She's not really a very good speaker, Ann thought. But then, she has probably given essentially the same speech innumerable times, in America as well as in England and Scotland. And in fact one should admire her indefatigable determination: in the face of all discouragement, and accusations of being a 'sell-out' - here she is, continuing to advocate working for peace. - But isn't the present about as bad as any time could be? What's the point of still trying to convince anybody that diplomacy has any chance of success now? We know we're going to have to endure war! How many will survive this time? What social and political values will survive, what defence for democracy in the face of confusion, loss, anger, fear?

During the muted applause after the speech ended, Ann realised she had actually heard very little of it. My mind is troubled, she told herself – there's too much to consider, and too little time or opportunity for consideration. Meg, Will, Peter - And worrying about my Father too, and my future.

There were a few questions that nobody there could have answered – especially Why is nothing warlike actually happening? Is this really a 'phoney war' now, as some people are calling it? - and if so, How long is it likely to last, before we're attacked and bombs begin to fall?

Jane thanked the Speaker for her 'brave and inspiring speech' and then the small crowd filed out almost silently.

Ann approached the Speaker and said what she knew were expected words: 'Thank you very much for all you said – you have given us great encouragement to continue the struggle for peace.'

'Thank you. I hope so' was the expected answer.

But then 'Yes, you *are* the young woman, aren't you - the ex-nurse – who served like me as a V.A.D. in the last war? We spoke on the ship from New York. I have wondered what – It was so strange, wasn't it? Frightening and inexplicable. It seems we were fortunate to survive – but what exactly happened, a U-boat attack, a collision with a submarine, who knows? – and in the middle of the night. I was told that no announcement would come from the Admiralty and it would be better just to forget about it – and in the present circumstances maybe that *is* the best thing to do – my husband here thinks so, don't you, dear?' He nodded.

She turned again to Ann. 'I'm saying this, and please don't repeat it, because I assume you were just as much puzzled and troubled by that event as I was. All in all, it seems very possible to me that we were lucky to survive. If the other ship had not been nearby – well, it's likely all or most of us would have drowned. In the middle of the night. In freezing cold water. My husband lost the manuscript of an important book he is writing. But we survived. So I think we should make use of the exceptional good fortune that saved us, and try to justify it in any way we can, especially by working for peace – even when that seems pointless. I am so relieved, even though we miss him terribly, that my eleven-year-old son is now with friends in America, so he can't be imprisoned and tortured as many of us, certainly including myself, will be, if the Nazis, as many seem to expect, do invade England. That's what I tell my husband. Who I see is looking at his watch and is about to say -'

He smiled grimly. '- that we must go, my dear. Otherwise we'll miss the train.'

The Vicar's wife came forward to accompany the Speaker and her husband to the station.

Meg and Ann stayed to help in clearing-up. When order was fully restored to the shabby room, 'Don't forget your knapsack, Ann' Meg reminded her, with an ironic smile. Then Jane drove them to Crab-apple Cottage.

On the way, she said quietly to Ann 'Can we meet briefly tomorrow, after lunch? I'm assuming you'll catch the 4:15. My flat is right beside the Library – Mum will give you directions.'

'Thank you. I guess I can be with you by about 1:30. And I'd like to walk, so please don't tell Mr Fortune.'

Fifteen

Yes, Ann thought as she lay in bed next morning, while the cock crowed perfunctorily, and she could hear the distant quarreling of the hens as Meg fed them and snagged their eggs, Yes, this is a life I could live. Maybe Daddy could come here too, and we could rent a house in Street – but then a sharp memory of Hilda's frowning face restored reality, and Ann set about washing and dressing to face the day – yet another cool calm day, she noted with pleasure. Rain later, perhaps.

As they sat drinking tea, after a breakfast of porridge and boiled egg, Meg said abruptly 'I must ask you more about Will, my dear. You mentioned having dinner with him after your last visit to us. – How did he seem? It may seem strange that I ask, but, Ann, he may not have told you this, but he seems to have cut himself off from us – from his sisters, from me. It's well over a year since he was last here. Obviously something is troubling him – maybe something I said, you know how thoughtless I am – or maybe a quarrel with his sisters; but they seem just as puzzled as I am. He was never good at remembering birthdays but - Maybe Jane will be able to tell you something if you get a chance to ask her. Or maybe he's said something to you? If it was a confidence, of course I don't want you to say anything. But it's so puzzling – and, I must admit, hurtful as well as worrying – especially as we hear about German bombing –'

Meg paused and blew her nose gently before continuing. 'Of course I'm not asking you to spy, or break a confidence.'

Uncomfortable, Ann replied 'I'm so sorry, Meg. He hasn't said anything to me, but I did pick up some reticence about you and Jane and Emily. I wouldn't want to cause any difficulty for any of you, but if you'd like me to -'

'Yes. I *would* like that, dear Ann. If you get the chance. And tell him, please, that we're not angry, just puzzled and sad – and how much we'd like to see him – how we love him and think about old times – and if there's a problem, how we'd like to -' Meg stopped abruptly, in tears. 'Sorry, sorry – that's just me -'

After breakfast, Ann again helped with feeding the hens and animals. Then went for a walk, accompanied by an eager yapping Skippy. I really need some good exercise, she told herself. And, thinking of the map Meg had laid out for Peter - I'd like to walk as far as the other two Clumps. She saw that the excitable little dog might be a problem; but he again ran off on a tangential path which, Ann realised, would lead him back to the Cottage. So she walked on as fast as she could, down to the river, and found a way across it on a narrow bridge.

But I'm truly out of practice, she told herself - why so breathless? And she decided to curtail her intended walk; but was still able to climb halfway up the nearer of the two Clumps, making her way past incurious cows, until she could look back towards Crab-apple Farm. A landscape so peaceful under the calm sun and cloudless sky, so verdant - 'England's green and pleasant land', yes, but do I belong here, could I ever belong here? And she began her return walk.

Near the bridge, she encountered a fisherman about to cast his fishing-line. As she approached, he called out 'Lovely day, Miss!' and she responded 'Oh, yes it is!'

'You from hereabouts?'

'Just visiting from London. So calm and beautiful here. And the countryside, so - lovely.'

'For the moment, but it won't last. Jerry is busy attacking elsewhere now, but soon, you wait, his bombs will be raining down on us. I read in yesterday's paper that right here we could be on Jerry's flight-path to London. Maybe you don't remember me from last night? I saw you with Mrs Avery, a real nice lady she is – her husband died in the last war, I knew him quite well, we used to see each other in the pub – and he had no need to go off and fight, he was over forty like me, but he volunteered, said he had to fight for King and Country, every able-bodied man should fight for King and Country. But my wife, she said No to me, we had four little ones, so – But I shouldn't be gossiping like this – Sorry, I hope you're not in a hurry - If my wife was alive she'd say "Now, Jim -" So, what did you think of the talk last night?'

'Oh.' Ann was suddenly reluctant to converse further. 'Oh, I guess we can only hope -'

'There! I knew it! I said to the wife you looked like an American. Someone said in the pub last night that Mrs Avery had an American visitor. So do you think your President will support us and fight against Jerry?'

'Oh, I'm not political, I was just a nurse, in the First War, I mean – And I'm a Canadian, not an American. And, I hope you'll excuse me, I'm going to be late if I don't hurry.'

'Sorry to delay you, my dear. But thanks for the chat. Now I'll see if the fish have anything to communicate to me. I think they know more than we think' and he laughed loudly as he cast his line.

Ann hurried on, realising that she might be late reaching Crab-apple Cottage and then, after lunch, Jane.

As she reached the Cottage, Meg called out from the kitchen 'The Hospital has just called, Ann.'

'Oh. Do they want me to hurry back?'

'No, but quite soon. I explained that you had planned to have tea with Jane, and they said that if you could get to the Hospital by late-afternoon, that would probably be fine – apparently your Father has had to be given more drugs, and is sleeping now, but before that he was calling again for you. So let's eat. I telephoned Jane to explain, so she knows you'll need to catch the 2:15. Did you have a good walk?'

'Yes. Lovely. But I'll just get my knapsack, and tidy up a bit. Oh, I hope -'

They chatted over tea and sandwiches, Ann enthusiastic about the countryside, the view from the Clump – 'and I had a chat with an interesting old man who was fishing near the bridge, he said he knew you.'

'Oh, we all know each other, Ann, if we've lived here long enough - and if it was old Sarson, then yes, we're old acquaintances, a nice man, he's a widower, his wife died recently, four children, all grown up and gone away, two went to Australia – see, we know whatever's going on. And *you'll* have to be going on soon, my dear, Jane will be waiting. And don't leave your knapsack behind! Thank you for coming. Who will feed the chickens now? Come back soon!'

Sixteen

When Ann reached the Street Library, a little breathless in the sharpening heat, Jane appeared immediately.

'Hullo, Ann. Where do you think I live? Can you guess?'

'In the Library?'

'Oh, no – then I'd never escape the books! So - not exactly. Follow me' and she led the way round the Library building to a flight of wooden stairs that ended one storey up, at a blue-painted door. 'Please admire my abode, Ann. Up here I could probably tell immediately if any thief entered the Library in a nefarious desire to purloin my Jane Austens – though I do wish the local children were avid readers of the classics – I advertise our wares in the local primary school every term, but alas they seem to prefer the garish offerings of the local cinema, so it's quite a challenge -' She stopped talking when she reached her front door, and waited for Ann to catch up. 'Now turn, dear Ann, and look at my view of Crab-apple Cottage – or, rather, of the Clump, though the new buildings get a little in the way – but isn't it a lovely view? Now come in and admire my little flat, we'll have a cuppa, as Mum would say, or rather two cuppas, one each. Don't mind Cat – she'll move, she knows she's always in the way and that she won't get her supper if she doesn't move. So choose a chair, Ann – I know you don't have much time, Mum phoned to say that the Hospital wanted you back A.S.A.P., apparently your Father – well, I told her I'd make sure you catch the 2:15 – and that gives us only an hour.' As she placed a tray near what was clearly *her* chair, she leaned for a moment towards Ann. 'And I have something I must talk to you about.'

Ann sat in smiling silence, sipping her cup of tea.

'So what do you think it is? Well, I won't make you guess. That wouldn't be fair. It's about Will. In fact, Mum said she would talk to you if there was time, and maybe she has. But she wouldn't be forceful like me – and Emily would be even more forceful, but of course she is preoccupied with the two boys, who run a bit wild, I think, and you've met her husband, haven't you, Roger? he doesn't like disciplining the boys, leaves that to Emily, and as I say she's always busy with this and that.'

'Yes' Ann responded, remembering Emily's visit, with husband and sons, 'boys can be rough, can't they? You and Emily were always so gentle, I remember.'

'Oh, we would have our fights, about who could bath first, or who would sit next to Dad, and then when you – But I mustn't ramble on, we don't have a lot of time. More tea? No? Well, as I said, it's about Will. We're all worried about him, and Emily and I are really cross with him about staying away, and not communicating at all with us, or even with Mum, and she tries so hard to keep in touch, as you probably know. She told him about you coming, and apparently he just said "Why?" and refused to come here to meet you when she asked him to, and he point-blank refuses to communicate with Emily and me, and we try not to feel angry and bitter -'

'Yes. I'm sorry about that. I've only had one conversation with him – after he came to visit my Father, who's in hospital after two heart attacks – I thought that was very kind of him, even though his flat is near the hospital – and his Store is quite near too, he said – anyway, I'll call him -'

'Call him? You mean you'll go to the shop where he works, and ask for him? Of course, he's never invited us there, except Mum, once, over a year ago, and she said he wanted to talk only about the shop and about the huge responsibilities of his job there. After that, Emily and I were so angry, and apparently he didn't ask Mum anything about us and didn't even suggest that we visit him in London, and of course he never remembers our birthdays, on purpose we think -'

Ann looked at her watch. 'I think maybe I'd better go soon, Jane. Thank you for the tea and sandwiches. I'll certainly talk to Will when I see him, and – urge him to contact you all - by 'phone, that would be easiest, wouldn't it?'

'Oh, and Ann, there's the War too, what if London's bombed? Or they say maybe the Germans will invade. What we heard last night, in that talk, it was speculation as she said, but if it happens the Germans might come right through here, they might land at Southampton or – And who knows what will happen? Anyway, I know you must go, but please, if you can – Mum and Emily and I would be so grateful. And I hope you have a good journey and find your Father very happy, and I hope you can come back soon and we can have more time to talk – I do get lonely in spite of the Readers, who are mostly very kind, and Mum and Emily – and we have so many happy memories of our time together with you, before that War, even though there was also sadness and misunderstanding –

and especially Dad being killed – oh, now I shouldn't have mentioned that, and just as you're going – but there was also so much happiness, as I said, truly happy memories, I know Emily feels the same – Oh, and what about Christmas? Only a few weeks away! This year it's hard to feel Christmassy, but – Mum's probably already talked to you about coming – Emily does the main meal and I do the sweets -'

'Thank you very much, Jane. Yes, Meg did mention Christmas - but she knows that I'll want to be with my Father, and I doubt if he'd be allowed to leave the Hospital, and if he did, his wife would probably – Also I know I'll be needed for extra duties, because so many nurses will want to be with their families. Anyway - It's been lovely to have time with you, Jane. Thank you for the tea.'

And Ann was glad to make her escape.

Seventeen

It was dusk when Ann reached the Hospital. Standing at the entrance was Will – who took her hand and led her inside. 'Come and sit down for a moment, Ann' he said, drawing her toward a bench.

They sat down together. Already she felt breathless with apprehension. 'It's Dad?' she whispered after a moment.

'Yes' he responded quietly. 'They couldn't reach you – you must have been on the train by then. Mum told them, and she gave them my number – I came right over, but Ann – I'm so sorry, I was too late to give him your love – and to tell him you were delayed. His wife and mother-in-law were there, just sitting in silence, you'll see them in a moment. One of the nurses told me they wouldn't move him before you came – so he's still there, you can see him and say goodbye.'

Ann sat in silence. Then tears came, and she turned towards Will, who leaned to embrace her. They sat together for a few more moments. Then she stood up, and, holding hands, they went along the passage towards her Father's room.

As she entered, Sybil turned a teary face towards Ann, who nodded to her, and then sat down on the edge of her Father's bed, took one of his flaccid hands in hers, and leaned forward far enough to kiss his cold rough cheek. 'Oh, Daddy' she whispered. 'Sorry I'm late. I love you. Goodbye.' His eyes were closed, his expression calm.

Afterwards she and Will remained briefly with Sybil and her mother, in the passage outside the room, so they could exchange telephone numbers. Sybil informed them that her husband had arranged all the details of his cremation and burial long ago - 'No service, and especially no hymns, that's what he said. That was his way. He didn't like the Church. Now I must take Mummy home.' And the two women walked away slowly.

'Come, let's eat' Will said.

At the restaurant, the proprietor bowed to Ann and murmured sympathy, as if he could tell, and perhaps he could, that she was bereaved. I'm not hungry, Ann told herself, but one should always eat, especially when distressed. So she sipped her wine, and smiled bleakly at Will.

'Well, in a way it's what I came for – I mean, to England, but I guess that doesn't make it any easier. Now I don't think I have any living relatives.'

'Not even in Canada? What about the wounded soldier, your cousin, didn't he have any siblings?'

'No. He was an only child, and *his* father was *my* father's only sibling. Daddy emigrated to Canada to join his brother to farm in the West, but it didn't work out – they quarrelled and Daddy went East to Ontario, where he married my Mother, but that didn't work out either, in the end – she left him, and remarried, and Daddy came back to England, and after a few years I followed him – my Mother died soon after the War ended and anyway she and my stepfather had made it clear that they didn't want me – or that's what I thought, though I wondered later, especially after she died, if I'd been unfair to them. Anyway, Daddy was remarried by then and - so I had to find my own way over here – and I was already training as a nurse when the War broke out. But I had met your Father before that, and then your Mother and you and the girls. So now I've told you the sad story of my life so far. Your turn.'

Will was glad he had got her talking, and he followed her life account with his - at intervals while they ate. 'But' he said 'you already know most of my story – at least until you abandoned us and rushed home to Canada.'

'Oh, Will' she responded, 'don't tease me. Especially not tonight.'

'Right, madame. Or mademoiselle. No, you *are* a married woman. Or were. Mum said you told her you actually *married* your cousin, the Canadian soldier who was badly wounded -'

'Yes. He was wounded during the Second Battle of Ypres. During that battle the Germans used poison gas for the first time – and many Canadian soldiers were killed, thousands I think, but also there were many others, like my cousin, who lived on with a lot of suffering. And he was also blinded. It was such a shock to come across him in the hospital where I was nursing, in London - to see his name on the list, and realise he was the Canadian cousin Daddy had told me about – who had actually contacted Daddy when he was in England training with the Canadian Army, that's what Daddy told me - before they were sent across to France. So I nursed him – as well as so many other wounded Canadian soldiers, and other Allied soldiers – and then he begged me to marry him. And at first – well, it's very complicated. Of course Davey was married and had a family, and even before he was killed I knew my love for him was – Well, he could never have married me, even if he'd wanted to, and I don't think he did. And of course there was your Mother, and you, and Jane and Emily – and I guess I thought it was better in the end, when he decided to be a soldier though he was really too old - and even before he went into the Army, I decided it was better for me to just go – get out of *his* life and *your* lives – So I did, rightly, or, probably, wrongly. And there was so much nursing to do in London as the War went on and the hospitals filled with more and more wounded soldiers. We were all just exhausted most of the time, we nurses.'

She paused, looked into his eyes, and then 'Was I wrong, Will – do you think I was wrong? You know, I think I'm a little drunk, all this wine you keep giving me.'

'No, I don't think you were wrong. It was an impossible situation for you. You were in love with Dad, as you said – even I could see that. But – It was a bit like your namesake's dilemma in, I can never remember the name of that novel by Jane Austen – oh yes, *Persuasion.* We had to read it at school – a strange introduction to Jane Austen, I think, for rambunctious boys, why not *Pride and Prejudice*? - but our English Master was a strange bird.

'But now for *my* confession, maybe *I've* had too much to drink too. Did you never realise that *I* was in love with you? A silly adolescent boy. Seems to me, looking back, that I was always yearning for you to notice me – but you only had eyes for Dad – Anyone could see you loved him, but it was so *unfair* – I won't groan on about that, don't worry – I sort of got over it, and I'll tell you about that another time, how I got over it, if you're interested. - But I forgot I wanted to ask you about Dad's poetry. You must have known about all his book-illustrations, he was admired for them, even though he made hardly any money from them, we were always close to penury - but he didn't seem to care unless there was a really severe shortage of money – and then he would illustrate another book, or Mum would beg a few pounds from her father, my grandfather, in Street. Or from one of her uncles.

'But – see, *I'm* getting drunk too - Did you know he wrote quite a lot of poetry in the years before the War, and then during the War too? Before the Army accepted him - he was over forty, and he wrote poems about what the War meant to people in England who just had to carry on, farmers and factory-workers, and women in munitions-factories, while things got worse and worse. I have wondered whether he went to fight in the War because he wanted to paint and write poetry about *that*, something different, something dangerous – and because of the suffering of the soldiers too - I think he did, even though he was killed so soon after he got back there after his Leave. I don't know if his poetry was any good, I only saw a couple of his poems, which he showed me when he was on leave in 1917, but he really cared about it – and the war, and his fellow soldiers, and their suffering - But what I was wanting to say – See, I'm almost as drunk as you, and we both better get to bed soon – What I was saying was that Mum has all his poetry, and his letters, what he wrote before he went, and what he wrote at the Front, and she won't let us see most of it. When she was asked to submit some of it to be considered for publication, she flat-out refused, just *refused*. And got angry if I asked about it, and wanted to see it. And she'd also insist that his war paintings and sketches were much more important than anything he wrote – that's where his talent lay, she'd say, and that was *his* opinion too, she'd say. My mother is a very determined lady. Don't be fooled by her, Ann. And I think she doesn't always understand *herself*, why she does some things, and won't do some other things. But I'm *not* going to let her keep Dad's poems and letters to herself. She has no right to do that. What do you think?'

Ann yawned, in spite of herself. 'Oh, Will, I'm just too tired to think. Can we talk about it tomorrow?'

He smiled, climbed rather shakily to his feet; and soon they were walking very carefully, arm in arm, towards his flat.

Ann, realising that she would be spending the night there, objected slurringly; but Will assured her that there were two beds and that they would each occupy one of them.

Oh, Meg, I'm so sorry. I'm so very sorry, to do this again – I realise how it will look - that in spite of all I've been saying, here I am again gone away without letting you know or explaining anything. If you are angry, of course I understand. I'll try to explain as well as I can here in this letter, but when I see you – soon, I hope, if you forgive me – I'll be able to give you a full explanation.

I think you probably know that Daddy died, last Sunday (he died just before I got to the hospital – also before Will was able to get there, after you called him). Will rushed there, but my stepmother told him he was too late. He waited for me and then I had a few minutes to say goodbye to Daddy. On Tuesday my stepmother called me (we had exchanged phone numbers) and told me to contact his lawyer, so I did and turns out that Daddy left quite a lot of money, most of it will go to Hilda of course but I will get enough the lawyer said to 'live very comfortably' (I didn't expect anything so I was quite surprised and very grateful). Oh but I should have said before that Will insisted on taking me to dinner after I said goodbye to Daddy and really if it wasn't for him I think I would have felt suicidal – he is very kind, I'll never forget his kindness. Then he also said he had some holiday-time due (he didn't take any earlier as he wanted to be sure the store would do well, and it did, in spite of War having been declared and people being worried even tho nothing much was happening) and so he said maybe we should go on a short holiday as he needed a break from the store and I needed a break after Daddy's death (there won't be a funeral, Hilda said, because Daddy didn't want one – he even put that in his Will).

So that's why we're here, for a few days! So many sad things happened at once, it was upsetting and exhausting. Will said we should get away for a few days, go to the West Country, which would be far from German bombing if that started, and he asked Did I have any special place I'd really like to go to and of course I said Lyme Regis! Because that's where Jane Austen set the most dramatic scene in 'Persuasion' (which is one of my favourite novels – the heroine is also called Ann! but spelt Anne). So here we are, actually staying in a 'bed-and-breakfast' in Uplyme, a village nearby. Not much sign of the War here (so far?). Just some 'vackies' (evacuated children) and a sort of air-raid shelter near the harbor, and such. We walked along the Cobb and Will persuaded me to jump down from it (like Louisa did in the novel) but of course he caught me (unlike Captain Wentworth who dropped Louisa!) so I didn't fall onto the stones and nearly die as she did. But I felt too sad to laugh. We also had a meal in a pub and drank to your health, and Jane's and Emily's (that reminded me of when we drank that wine the day I arrived and you were all so kind and welcoming!).

Sorry, this is a rushed and messy letter. I'm writing it in the late afternoon, Will is doing some "shop-work" (he says), lots of math it looks like - he called the store this morning to see how things were going. And then we are going! To the pub for supper, and tomorrow we'll be going back to London. (Did you know Will has a car, it's a blue Morris Minor, which he loves – he says we may drive to Edge!)

By the way, Will and I have also had some long talks, and he said that when we visit you, he and you can have some long conversations too!!! He says he and you have lots to talk about.

Meanwhile, Meg, please forgive me, and this hasty messy letter – I thought it would be better to write even if we get to talk before it even reaches you (I don't know how long the post takes in England now!) and I'll telephone anyway when we get to London.

So meanwhile Will and I send our love to you – Ann

Eighteen

'But why would she do that, Mum? Just disappear. I remember when Daddy died – when that telegram came – and we all just cried and cried, you and Jane and me – so I can guess how upset she would be, and you say the doctor you spoke to said it was just so unfortunate that he died suddenly in the end, with only his wife and mother-in-law there, so of course it must have been upsetting. But she should have considered us too. Did you try to talk to Will? Surely he should have 'phoned and let you know what happened, and why there was just no answer when you 'phoned him that night and yesterday? It all seems so odd. Roger thinks so too.'

Meg sighed. 'Well, looks as if we'll just have to wait a bit longer. I thought of contacting the Police, but I'm sure they're very busy, there's a war on, remember!'

'Yes, and that makes it all the more worrying, doesn't it?'

'But maybe we're worrying unnecessarily, Emmy. Anyway, one thing looks certain – that they're together, and *that* would be a good thing. We'll see. How are Roger and the boys?'

'Oh, I wasn't going to tell you when there's so much else to worry about – and you're certainly not to worry about it! And I've been warning them about it, and Roger has too, though I think that he also encourages them. But Michael fell out of a tree yesterday and we had to rush him to the hospital. He was very brave, hardly cried at all, but of course I was frantic with worry. And Roger was too. But the doctor there said it wasn't serious, he was lucky - no breaks, just bruises - but they would keep him there overnight for observation, just to be sure he's all right. So we can bring him home this afternoon. Maybe it will teach them both a lesson.'

'Oh, Emmy, what a worry! You should have told me and I could have come over and looked after Oliver at least. I hope Michael's fine now and maybe it will be a lesson for both of them about climbing trees.'

'Maybe. But boys will be boys! I must go now and cook the supper, Mum. Please let me know when you hear from Ann or Will. Actually I think – I can't help thinking -'

'I know what you're going to say, dear. Yes, and that may be a complication – but it may also be to the good if they're together – well, I think they *must* be together. And I'm sure we'll hear soon, from Ann if not from Will. By the way, don't you think it's strange, dear -?'

'What?'

'Michael and Oliver. Names. About names. For some reason, I just started thinking about names. It was Davey who insisted on *your* names, you three, and of course I accepted - they seemed nice enough names, Will and Jane and you, Emily. All great literary figures, he said – William Shakespeare and Jane Austen and Emily Bronte – his three most favourite writers. I don't know why that came back to me now. Maybe it's because I'm also thinking more about Davey, again, with Ann being here, and remembering all the loss and deaths and suffering in our generation – and now here we are, another time of war, unless something can still be done to prevent it all happening again, all that our generation suffered – all the terrible deaths, all that suffering. We heard about that again the other night from that woman Jane thinks so highly of, it was very depressing. She called us "The War Generation".'

'And not just *your* generation, Mum, though you had the worst of it. *We* had to suffer too, especially when Daddy was killed. Didn't we say these things when we were together just after Ann came back? I think so. And I suppose we'll be saying them again – and if *this* war goes on and on, we'll be desperate when we see that our sons will be swallowed by it too. But – oh, Mum, I'm sorry – you've got enough to worry about, both of us have – And I should get off the line, there may be a call from Ann, she may be trying to get through to you right now. So -'

'Yes. Thank you, Emily. I hope all is fine with Michael. Please let me know. Fortune will drive me round if I can help, with nursing or cooking. Meanwhile, goodbye.'

She put the phone down, and almost immediately it rang again. 'Hullo, hullo' she said (bellowed, she told herself - control yourself, Margaret!). But it wasn't Ann or Will.

'Mrs Avery? This is the Home. I'm so sorry to bother you, but we have a problem you or that young woman, Ann, is that her name? might be good enough to help us deal with. You'll remember Peter Arnold, you visited him recently. To cut a long story short, he has been upset, more and more upset, and tried to escape the grounds twice since your visit, in fact the second time was almost disastrous because he tried to cross a major highway and was almost killed by an army lorry, there are so many on the roads now and often speeding – Anyway, as I say, he has been increasingly troubled since your visit, and he constantly repeats Ann's name -'

'Oh, I'm so sorry, I'm just so glad he's safe again with you.'

'Yes, but we feel it might settle his mind – his health is deteriorating badly, the doctor says, because he won't eat properly or take his pills – It might help so much if you and especially your friend Ann can come here soon. We could tell him you were coming and that might help to settle his mind.'

'Of course we'll come, as soon as possible. But Ann is away at the moment and I'm not sure when I'll see her. As soon as I do, I'll telephone. Or my friend Martha will. I'm sorry I can't say more at this point. I could come on my own, but it was clear to me too that it's Ann he wants. If you can tell him that Ann sends her love and will soon visit him -'

'Yes, I'll do that, Mrs Avery, I'll tell him Ann will visit him as soon as possible.'

And then, ten minutes later, a third call.

This time, Meg could hear, faintly through a crackling on the line which suggested the call was long-distance, 'Meg? Meg? Can you hear me? It's Ann. I can't hear you, the line is too bad, but I hope you can hear *me*. IT'S ANN. We'll be with you soon, Will and I, maybe tonight, and then I'll explain everything. I'm so sorry for any worry I've caused you. Truly I am. Let me repeat – *Will and I will be with you a.s.a.p. and we send our love.* 'Bye for now.'

Nineteen

'So did you speak to her?' Will put a plate of fish-and-chips in front of her.

They were in the back garden of a pub, 'The Lamb and Falcon'. 'You're the Lamb' he'd said while parking the car in front of the pub, off the busy main road, 'so I'm the Falcon – what do falcons do apart from hunting smaller creatures? But I'd have thought a lamb might be a bit of a challenge unless it was a very small one? Oh, I'm still talking nonsense. You must be sick of me. But you're so quiet! Now I'll get my supper and a pint of very welcome and, I hope, very cold Bitter. How about you? Fish-and-chips with a half-pint?'

'No, just water. With fish-and-chips, if necessary - unless they have a Scotch pie or even Toad-in-the hole.'

He went inside to order their meal. As she waited for him, she turned over in her mind some memories, such very happy memories, of their brief holiday in Lyme Regis. I should feel guilty to have been so happy – Please forgive me, Daddy, for being happy so soon after you died. She looked up and smiled at Will as he put down a tray with her Scotch pie, and his Toad-in-the-hole and pint of Bitter.

'And now what?' he said cheerfully, turning to her. 'I've learnt in the last few days what that look means! So say your piece, Juliet!'

'Juliet? No, I'm no Juliet and you're no Romeo, Sir! Age *has* withered us. But at least we can hope to escape their fate, and maybe, remembering that the Montagues or Capulets are about to beat us all up, we will survive *this* great war. Does that make any sense? No, I don't think so.'

She glanced at him, smiling slightly. But his face was set in a sudden bitterness. Why – is he angry, or hurt - is this old pain or new? Did I say something -?

He sat still for a few minutes, not eating or drinking, and turned his face away from her. Then said softly 'The time has come. We've been living a dream these last few days. I didn't want it to end. I've never been so happy. Please believe that, Ann. Never! Never! But reality, reality, reality. We *must* talk. *I* must talk.'

There was a long silence while he drank and ate. Then he turned towards her again.

'Ann. Ann, I'm homosexual.'

She sat in silence for a moment, then leaned towards him and put an arm round his shoulders.

'Oh, Will. And I'm too old to have a baby. So all we can do is die, I guess?'

He laughed – a sudden guffaw. Then drained his glass, put their plates and utensils on the tray, stood up. 'Come on, let's go home. To Crab-apple Cottage, that's where we need to be. Oh, Ann -' as she stood and reached up to kiss him. 'Oh, Ann. I love you.'

Twenty

Meg was on the 'phone speaking to Jane. She had already spoken to Martha, telling her about Peter Arnold's situation - when the kitchen-door suddenly opened, Skippy started barking - and she turned, to see Ann and Will coming towards her. 'Oh' she said, 'Jane, I can't talk any more, they're -' She dropped the telephone as Ann and Will came to her and, one after the other, hugged her.

'Oh, what a fright you gave me, and there's Jane on the line, what will she think – Ann, please speak to her and say -' Meg sat down, and reached for Will, as Ann conversed briefly with Jane.

'I was just about to have some tea, the water's just boiled, so let's – Ann, could you make some tea while I tell my son what a lot of worry and trouble he's caused?'

'All right, Mum. I'm here now.' Will sat down beside her and took her hand. 'I'm sorry about all the – about my silence.'

'Well, I might forgive you if you promise not to stay away from us again. Your sisters have been very upset, of course. And me too. They wanted to visit you in London but were afraid of causing trouble, and with your wife and her children -'

'Mum, don't say any more now. There's a lot to explain, and I have to do that. And a lot of pain and confusion that I'll also have to talk about. Let's have our tea and then -'

'But you must be starving – it's nearly ten o'clock. Or did you have supper on the way?'

'Yes, we did. I couldn't eat any more now.'

'Nor could I' Ann said.

'So – help yourself to some tea if you want to. Oh, and are you going to stay the night? If so, I should -'

'Mum. Please, just listen. And yes, we would like to stay the night – but I must be back in London by tomorrow night. Ann too, I suppose – you'll have to sort some things out, won't you, Ann? Your accommodation – and at the Hospital?'

'But you must come back here, and stay as long as you like. I might say, too, that Skippy has been missing you, Ann, and of course I've had to feed Elsie, Horace and the pigs and sheep and chickens every day! We've *all* been missing you! But that's not the most important thing – I've just been talking again to Martha, and she thinks we should visit Peter Arnold tomorrow - It's a crisis, apparently – he has been calling out for you especially, Ann.'

Will looked hard at his Mother. 'Peter Arnold? Did you say "Peter Arnold"?'

'Yes. Why? His sister asked me to visit him with her because he knew Davey, apparently - before the First War – and he was gassed in the Battle of Ypres -'

'Yes. I knew him. He was a bit older than me, four years maybe, and he used to look out for Dad and walk with him, those long country walks Dad loved to go on - I went on a few, as you probably remember, but Dad made it increasingly clear that I was a nuisance, and I got badly lost once, and that frightened me, so I stopped – and anyway there was school and University Entrance, which I failed of course - you remember how upset Grandad was, he was paying for my schooling, that nasty little public-school - Anyway, sorry, I'm getting carried away. I just wanted to say that I knew Peter Arnold.'

Meg: 'So would you like to come with us? As I was saying, they told us, Martha and me – at the Home where he's living now – that he is in a bad way. Ann came with Martha and me last time, and Martha wants us to go again tomorrow, as I was saying.'

'Well, yes, I'll come. In fact, I'll drive you there. But I'll stay in the background. Maybe they won't want him to see me anyway.'

Meg got up suddenly. 'Look, you two – You must be exhausted, we'll have some time to talk tomorrow, and of course Jane and Emily will want to see you, Will, before you go back to London. So you must get some sleep. I'll put you in the small spare-room, Will -'

'Oh, no, Mum. Ann and I will sleep together in the old double-bed – you still have it, don't you?'

'But is that all right, Ann? My son is hardly to be trusted, you know. He could murder you in the night.'

'Oh, *Mum!* Now that's not funny. But you're right, we've slept in another double-bed, in a B&B in Uplyme, and neither of us murdered the other.'

'All right. I can see he has bullied you into submission, Ann. You don't say a word!'

'Because there's no need, dear Meg. He's a peaceful sleeper, although he does have the bad habit of throwing a leg or two over my stomach. But I'll try not to scream when he does that tonight. Good night, Meg. It's *lovely* to be in Crab-apple Cottage again.'

Twenty-one

They slept well, Will conceded. Meg brought them a tray with tea and fruit at about nine a.m. 'I let you sleep in a little, but you can hear Chantecleer, and he's shouting "Feed me and my hens, and then the rest of the crew!" So get on, get up, lazy ones, life's not waiting for you. And besides, I have lots of questions for you to answer.'

'Oh, go away' Will groaned.

Later, they sat in the garden, at the picnic-table, and Meg served tea before saying 'And now, let's talk. We haven't got long, the Girls are coming over, and then we'll be meeting Martha for lunch and going on to see poor Peter Arnold – that's the schedule for today. Any questions? Before you start answering *my* questions.'

Will: 'I'll drive us there, to the Home, and wait in the car while you visit Peter Arnold.'

'Good. Then we won't have to trouble Fortune at all. I'll let Martha know that we'll meet her for lunch in Street. And now, Will, Ann, who's going first?'

Will: 'Me. I. So you can get over the shock, Mum. I'll tell you just like I told Ann. I'm homosexual.'

Meg drew a deep breath. 'There. That's what Davey once told me he thought. Are you sure?'

'Yes, I'm sure. And that's one reason I – Well. And so I lied to you, and Jane and Emily. Which is why it would have been awkward for you to visit me in London.'

'You mean you never had a wife or even a woman friend with children?'

'Yes, I mean that, Mum. I'm sorry. I never did. If you had come to my flat you might have met Jeremy, who was my partner – we lived together for a while before he moved on – and he always called me a coward for deceiving you – and he was right, I was a coward, I *am* a coward.'

Ann: 'Oh, Will, don't be so hard on yourself.'

'Anyway, now I am Out. I told Ann yesterday, I'm telling you today, and I'll tell Jane and Emily too. And anyone else who wants to know *can* know, I'm fed up with keeping secrets. And Ann -'

Meg: 'Ann – what?'

Ann smiled. 'Ann accepts the situation. She loves Will as Will, as who he is, and I'm proud that he has decided to be exactly who God made him. And, Meg – as you know, I'm too old to have children. Maybe Will and I'll adopt children. We'll see. We haven't even discussed that – sorry, Will.'

Meg sighed – with pleasure or exasperation? 'My dear son, so all will be well now. Will it? I wondered – oh, I wondered about many things, as it seemed you were going further and further away from us. But all I can say now is: Congratulations. I love you both. Please be happy together. And while I think of it, will you two come to us for Christmas? You said it wouldn't be possible, Ann, because of nursing-duties and especially because of your father, you needed to be with him, in the hospital and of course we all understood – but I think Emily will be hosting Christmas Dinner, after of course the Service in our little local church, and Jane and I will do the pudding – We'll all be delighted if you – And it would get you both out of London, especially if the War actually gets going and the Nazis are bombing in earnest – as some people say they will be soon. And we all need to stick together and be positive, whatever happens. I know I'm being forward, Ann, and insensitive, but that's the way we are about important family occasions in this country, or at least in this corner of it – we like to be well organized in good time. And remember,

I have a very undependable son! But I'm gabbling again.'

Ann: 'Thank you so much, Meg. I wish I could commit, but I already agreed, a while back, to be on nursing support throughout Christmas and New Year – so many of the nurses have husbands and children and need a break, we have more and more badly-wounded coming in all the time. And Will and I want to get together as often as possible, in our favourite restaurant and pub. In fact, I'm going to move into his flat to be with him – did you know that, Will? And I'll see how things are in the Hospital as soon as I'm back nursing – Matron was very understanding about me needing some time away after Daddy's death, but -'

Meg: 'I understand. I'll tell the others, but you know that we would all miss you greatly. And of course things could have changed radically by then. In the War, I mean – it might actually have started! And now, I'll telephone Martha. Jane and Emily will be here soon. Emily's Michael had a fall the other day when he was climbing a tree, but, praise be, he's fine, just a few bruises and a good lesson to both boys. I think you knew about that, Ann? So I can say that all is well, better than well, with our family at present, praise the Lord. If only the war situation was also good - but it's not, the news is bad, bad, as you'll learn if you listen to the BBC News on the wireless. They say the Nazis will attack us soon, Hitler knows now that "We will *never* surrender", whatever he says or does. And of course they're invading France, and they can easily invade *us* from there. Sorry to cast a shadow. Now I'd better get on before the girls arrive – and you'd better prepare to explain and defend yourself, my dear son.'

'Just a moment, Mum. I've got one other thing to tell you – tell you both. I've been called-up. So I may not even be in London for Christmas.'

'Oh no' and Meg turned towards Ann. 'When? When will you have to go?'

Ann sat very still - shocked, dismayed, her happiness crumbling painfully. Why did he keep it secret from me? Then of course, like Meg's, her thoughts went quickly to Davey. And back to Will. No, please God – he can't go, I won't let him go. She turned sharply to him. 'No, Will – no, you're too old. They can't make you go. When did they -? Have you had a Medical exam? Did you tell them you don't believe in war?'

He smiled grimly. 'I'm younger than Dad was when *he* went. And yes, I don't believe in war – we had that long conversation in Lyme Regis, Ann, you and me, of course I remember that. And so many people are pacifists now – like that woman you told me about, who you met on the boat and then heard talking at a meeting in Street. But then I've been thinking, it doesn't matter what *I* think when my country is in danger. We haven't been attacked yet, but we will be. Any day now we will be. As Mum is saying. Mr Churchill has warned about that, over and over. Hitler and Mussolini, Nazis and Fascists - it's even worse than the Kaiser. And also, *I* haven't got a wife and children – I haven't got a family. Dad went to fight for his country even though he *did* have a family. I love you but -'

Meg: 'Oh, Will. Oh, Ann. What can I say? Sometimes it seems that the whole world is crumbling and only Evil is strong. But we must have hope. And any moment now, Jane and Emily will be here – I must put the kettle on and get myself ready, look at me in my shabby dress, and we don't have a lot of time before meeting Martha -'

She bustled off into the cottage. Will looked across at Ann and smiled thinly – with relief, she thought. Or embarrasment. She stared back at him. Am I angry? Or just disturbed, confused.

Twenty-two

'Coo-ee! Coo-ee!'

Jane and Emily appeared round the side of the Cottage. Will stood up to greet them, and then embraced them stiffly in turn. Then they all four sat down in silence, and almost immediately Meg appeared with a tray bearing tea-pot, cups and saucers, and sandwiches. 'There you are! Right on time too. So what do you think of our returning Good Samaritan – I mean Prodigal Son? And how is Michael, Emily? Boys! I hope they've both learnt a valuable lesson.'

Emily laughed briefly, then turned to Will. 'I won't say we haven't been puzzled and upset, Will – Roger and me, and even the boys – but as Mum would say, wouldn't you, Mum? better to let bygones be bygones and move on, especially as things are generally so bad, and have been for a while, what with the Depression especially and now this War, and who knows how things will turn out. Roger says that we just have to soldier on and try to make the best of things, and that's how I think too.'

There was another long pause before Jane cleared her throat and said haltingly 'Well, but we're so glad that we are all together again and I hope that we can all be good friends again, especially for Mum's sake.'

After that, they were able to laugh at some remembered humorous incidents; and by the time they all had to leave as lunch-time approached, Ann felt that good relations had been restored, however tenuously. But the topics of Will's homosexuality and war-service had not been addressed, she noted.

Meg and Ann climbed into Will's little Morris Minor, parked near the entrance like Emily's vehicle, and they set off for Street, arriving at the restaurant a few minutes late. Martha was already there. They had a quick light lunch together. 'I'll drive us there if the three of you can fit into my little car' Will announced, and tactfully 'You'll have to guide me, Martha, so could you sit in the front?'

When they arrived and were admitted into the big grey building, they were led to the Mother Superior's office. 'He is not in a good state, I am informed' she said. 'But he has made it clear that he wishes to see Ann – that's you, I assume' she said, glancing at Ann, 'and he also seemed to be saying your name, young man, if you are William, yes – so I think you two should spend a short time with him, and then you two ladies, if he is still in a good state. And I have an item that he wishes you to have, Ann – a satchel that appears to contain manuscript material – here it is' and she handed it to Ann. 'You can take it in with you, so he can see that his wish is fulfilled. Please follow Sister now.'

They found Peter Arnold lying in his bed, with his eyes closed. He was breathing stertorously. The Minder smiled thinly at them, then said quite loudly 'Peter? Peter? Your visitors are here. You remember they were coming, and you said you wanted to see Ann, that's your name isn't it? And who is your companion? William. It's *Ann and William.*'

Peter opened his eyes flickeringly. He tried to smile. But clearly he was now incapable of even a fitful response. Ann and Will waited a few minutes, calling 'Peter?' gently a few times before the Minder shrugged and whispered 'Sorry, I don't think he can respond, he's too weak now'. So they each said 'Goodbye, Peter' and Ann added 'Our love and prayers are with you.'

As they left his bedside, Martha came in, and remained for about ten minutes sitting at the bedside, holding his hands, and whispering a final farewell to the half-brother who had only recently come back into her life.

On the way home, Martha broke the silence to thank them for visiting Peter. 'He was always a lost soul, that's what his mother told me, but maybe now he will find rest. Thank you all for visiting him.'

Ann was clutching the satchel. What can be in it? she wondered. It's quite heavy, but I think it's all paper.

And 'all paper' is what it was. But Ann, whose memory of the young Peter Arnold was far from clear, thought she remembered the satchel itself; Martha said she had never seen it before; and Will, after a meditative silence while driving them home, suddenly remarked that Yes, he did remember it, he remembered it well. 'And I think I know what's in it.'

Martha telephoned next day to say that Peter Arnold had died during the night, and would be cremated. 'No service, just a small immediate-family gathering - his mother, stepmother I mean, said she couldn't face the strain, and from what I saw of her, that's totally understandable.'

Meanwhile, Jane had examined the contents of the satchel. 'It's a novel, set in the Great War, but I'm afraid the text is almost impossible to read, his writing was dreadful but also the ink is very faint and the paper disintegrating. *But* there are some letters, to him, and by him, rather better preserved, and manuscripts of poetry, which might be important. And some sketches, war scenes. And some of the poetry is not by him but by Dad – his writing was very idiosyncratic, Dad's I mean, as I'm sure we all remember – Which raises the question, obviously, about how poems by Dad got among Peter Arnold's writing. And was he a painter, like Dad? Are the sketches by him or by Dad, or by both of them?'

When Meg communicated Jane's comments to Will – he and Ann had driven to London after the abortive visit to Peter Arnold, and a quick supper – he responded by saying that they would be back at Crab-apple Cottage the next weekend, and then all of the family could discuss the satchel's contents. But meanwhile Meg had herself looked through them, and was excited and troubled by what she found. Many of the poetry texts duplicated poems Davey had sent her in 1916–17, and some of the letters were first drafts of letters he had written her. Did she feel that her privacy had been violated, she asked herself? And remembered all Will's pleas that she allow the poems to be published.

Another problem surfaced almost simultaneously. Yes, Jane was happy and fulfilled as a librarian – wasn't she? Wasn't she? But Emily and Roger and the boys – Increasingly Emily had been saying that, even in its reduced state, Crab-apple Farm was far too much work for one person ('for one old woman' Meg translated, with a flash of irritation). But maybe Emily was right, it was all getting a bit heavy, demanding, otherwise why was she so grateful for Ann's help? Yes, she was still fit, but also increasingly out of breath as she climbed up the path to the Cottage.

And what a lovely place this Farm would be for the boys to grow up in, as she had grown up – and her own children. Surely she shouldn't deny that happiness to them? But then, where would *she* go? Yes, it's a problem, but one I should try to deal with. Come on, old woman! And she smiled as she looked, again, at her image in the hall mirror.

Twenty-three

It was a few months later. Jane telephoned Meg. 'Are you busy, Mum? Can I come over?'

When she arrived, Meg was busy pruning apple-trees - "I'm late this year, I'm getting lazy" she called down to Jane - who, troubled to see Meg balancing on a swaying ladder, suddenly recalled helping her, a vigorous woman in her prime, by gathering apples for sale at the market. Enveloped in Meg's old apron, little Jane would run about catching apples as Meg threw them down to her. But now memories of that game underlined her mother's obvious physical decline. Mum's really growing old now, Jane told herself, she really should marry Mr Fortune next time he asks her – it was a family joke that he asked twice a year, at Easter and Christmas.

'I think that's enough physical activity for an old body' Meg said finally. 'Time for tea.'

Later, sitting in the shade of the old oak, with the tea-things deployed, she asked 'So what is this about, Jane? I hope everything's going well in the Library?'

'Oh, yes. Number of readers improving, fewer lost or damaged books.'

'Good. So it must be family matters?'

'Yes, Mum. That satchel, from Peter Arnold – I've gone carefully through the contents, including Dad's letters to you, and his poems. He's - really a good poet, I think. But, as you know, none of these are his War-poetry. *You* have all of those.'

'Yes. He sent them to me, just before he was killed. And with the poems was a letter saying, among other things, that *none* of his poems should ever be published without his permission and revision. That was his wish – his last wish – and of course I have respected it. At one point, when they were setting up his War-art for that exhibition, which will be finishing soon I think, I thought of just burning all his poems and letters

– and sometimes I'm sorry I didn't. Those people at the War Museum just wouldn't let me alone until I told them I had already burnt some of them and was thinking of burning them all – I hadn't, and wouldn't, but, thank goodness, that threat really worked.'

'But, Mum, some copies, probably early versions, of his poems are in the satchel – as well as first-drafts of letters, some to you and some to – other people. People, men, he knew as comrades in the War – or, like Peter Arnold, after meeting them while walking before the War, or in pubs, or in the Army, fellow officers or – servants, they had servants. Oh, Mum, this is so complicated to understand or explain. What I wanted to say mainly is that some, many, of the texts you have refused to allow to be published – well, that they exist, or some of them do, versions of them, even originals – so it's tricky. I know what *I* think -'

'Well, what *do* you think? I'm just an old woman with old-fashioned ideas who tries to do the right thing, how can *I* know what's right?'

'Well - What I think is that you should allow any and all of Dad's writing to be published. He didn't absolutely prohibit publication, did he? And even if he did, he didn't know it was his last word, that he was going to be killed. Maybe he didn't know how good, even *great*, his war-poetry is. It may be too late now anyway, until after this War is over – there's a shortage of paper, and publishers are having to retrench. Oh, Mum – I'm sorry about all this worry, when there's more than enough to worry about anyway. But I thought, if I didn't talk to you about this -'

'It's all right, Jane. Don't be troubled by me. I think we should work it out as a family. We can have a Family Conference, like the one when Davey told us he was going to volunteer to fight – and eventually, remember? he persuaded us to accept his decision. I'll telephone Will and ask him to be sure to come soon, the sooner the better, and you talk to Emmy. And now I must see to the chickens, I hope they've produced enough eggs for me to sell tomorrow at the market - thank you very much for your help, dear Jane.'

Twenty-four

Meg: 'Hullo, Ann? I'm glad you've answered because I've been wanting to remember to tell you that your letter from Lyme Regis arrived safely, some time ago. Sorry I forgot to mention it. Maybe because we haven't seen you for a while. Hope you can hear me? I was interested in all you said about Lyme Regis, and I do remember that scene in *Persuasion*, when Louisa jumps from the Cobb and Wentworth doesn't catch her (I remember wondering if he really did that on purpose? but that would be a mean thing to do - and he was the Hero!). I suppose you are now very busy working as a nurse again, in the hospital where your Father died. Will told me that. Sometimes I can get him on his office-phone when I can't get through otherwise. Is he there by any chance?'

'No, he's at a meeting. I'll ask him to call you as soon as he gets in. Yes, I can hear you – just about. Yes, I'm a nurse again. I was interviewed by the Matron, but when I said I'd been a V.A.D. in the last War she said immediately that, Yes, they needed, and will need, all the experienced help they can get. And of course I was already known in the hospital through helping while Daddy was a patient there. So I don't know when I might be able to get to Crab-apple Cottage. Hopefully soon!'

'HULLO! Meg again! Just to say goodbye and good wishes from all of us here. 'Bye! Oh, one last thing – I must tell you and Will that I may be moving soon, Emily and Roger have suggested that we exchange houses for a while, and see how it works, but I think it will be very good for the two boys, don't you? They love it here at the Cottage. So, goodbye.'

Ann put down the phone with a sigh. She wasn't yet used to sleeping during the day, and found it difficult to stay awake through the night, so Meg's call had been intrusive. She decided to make herself a pot of tea – Will's going to be back soon, and we'll probably go out for a pub-supper.

When he came in, half-an-hour later, she retailed Meg's news and he commented desultorily.

'It's been a varied day' he sighed. 'First, two Staff resigned - one is moving away from London, worried about the bombing, she says – I said What bombing? and she said It's coming and it'll be terrible, I read an article about it - And the other is emigrating to Australia, though I wonder if his boat will sail. Second, I've got an appointment with my doctor and next day with a Military Board - as I'm going on for forty, they want to have a close look at me. How about you?'

'Well, quite a busy day in the Hospital, mainly fetching and carrying for Matron, who seems to be as lazy as they come. And I get tired and irritable – but that's only until I get used to night-duty again, I think. Oh, and Meg wants us to come for a Family Debate or something - about those poems of your Father's, and also she said she's thinking of giving up Crab-tree Cottage, or rather something about exchanging it with Emily and Roger, for during the War - the boys would love living there, she said

– but I wonder what you think, and of course we don't know how long the War will last anyway.'

'I think it's their business and I don't know why they want to drag the rest of us into it. But I do think we need to decide about the poetry – Dad's and Peter Arnold's. Mum has held onto Dad's letters and poems so long, why all the secrecy? that it's a real problem for her now, so maybe we can help her decide – especially if she's going to move to Street, she'll need to sort out her things - but I wonder about that, Roger's not very dependable. Well, we'll see – quite a lot to work out and, I warn you, quite a chance of a family row. '

'Oh. Well, Jane said she would consult a teacher in the primary school who has published a lot of poetry, so at least there could be a quick solution on that item! Now – ready to go to the pub for your pint of Bitter with fish-and-chips – which I've decided to avoid when possible, but what else do they serve now?'

'Yes, let's go and get drunk, in honour of – Ann, do you know the date today?'

'23rd of April, isn't it?'

'Yes, and why is that date significant?'

'Oh – You tell me.'

'Oh, Ann, I'm disappointed in you. 23rd of April: St George's Day – you wouldn't know, but he is, was, the patron saint of England. But more: Death-day, I think, of Rupert Brooke; birth-day and death-day of William Shakespeare, after whom I am named. And why does that matter? Because today is the 23rd of April which is also *my* birthday, of course - my 39th birthday. I'm surprised that Mum and Jane and Emily have forgotten. Maybe they've lost patience with me! But, you will say, why does it matter? And you're right, it doesn't, so kiss me and that will be a most acceptable birthday-present, my dear Ann. And after that, tell me the date of your birthday, just in case I ever manage to remember it.'

Twenty-five

'Only just made it!' Ann appeared outside the window of the compartment. 'I'm breathless, which shows that I need more real exercise – going round the ward or running to fulfill Matron's orders is clearly not enough. So let's walk to the Cottage, when we get to Street – I really need a good walk, and it's another lovely day! A real Spring day! And I hope Mr Fortune doesn't know we're coming.' Ann kissed Will lightly on the cheek.

'Not a lovely day if you live in Europe and the Nazis are murdering Jews and homosexuals and other helpless people everywhere you look – or try not to look. But I shouldn't be facetious – it's horrific, it's appalling, and all we seem able to do is read about it.' Will put his *Times* aside. He and Ann had their second-class compartment to themselves, though there were young men in military uniform in several of the other carriages; so he felt free to talk quite loudly.

The conductor suddenly appeared, to check and punch their tickets. 'Lovely day!' he noted cheerfully.

'Oh – yes it is' Will responded, feeling momentarily hypocritical. And the train rumbled on, swaying and racketing.

As they set off for Crab-apple Farm, Ann said: 'You know, it'll soon be a year since I last did this walk – or tried to, Mr Fortune waylaid me and drove me to the Cottage gate. Such a nice man' she continued. 'I don't understand why -'

'Of course you do! It's the bloody English class-system. I've tried and tried to get Mum to respond to him as a real live human-being – not a servile member of the lower class – and of course I got nowhere. And *he's* just as bad. *She* thinks of him, in spite of all he's done, even saving the Farm for her, with money she has probably never repaid, after Dad died - her own father had died a few years earlier, before the War, did I tell you? leaving a large mysterious debt for her to pay – and yet she thinks of Fortune as a mere serf, and *he* adores her as the Queen of Hearts - but I'm getting breathless, Ann, I'm not in good condition like you, I don't have to gallop about to serve Matron, I mostly just sit at my desk and ask when the tea's going to arrive – Oh, don't listen to me – you're supposed to be saying, every few minutes, Isn't it a *lovely* day, did you hear that *robin*, aren't those daffodils *glorious* -'

Ann smiled. 'Well, at least we're having fun, or trying to have fun, on this beautiful day. I hope the others are too.'

'Oh, but I *am* being serious.'

As they climbed the path towards the Cottage, Ann said suddenly 'Do you remember that old apple-tree, the one that used to stand near the back-door, outside the kitchen-window?'

'Yes. It was blown down in a storm, was it fifteen years ago? Yes, I remember climbing it when I was a boy. I loved that old tree.'

'I did too.' She stopped for a moment. Then walked on slowly behind

Will towards the kitchen-door, thinking I nearly said it, I nearly *had* to say it, That's where your Father kissed me – that's where your Father kissed me!

Meg suddenly appeared in the doorway. 'Oh, I thought I heard – Come in, I'm so glad you're early, you're the first – we'll sit and have tea and a chat -'

'Mum, we're early because we'll need to leave straight after lunch, Ann's on duty tonight and she'll need a sleep before that. But it's good to see you. How is everybody?'

'Well, as far as I know, all fine. I think you know Michael's fully recovered, he's playing cricket again. We'll all sit outside, it's such a lovely day. Can you help me bring some more chairs out?'

And soon they were sitting – Meg, Ann and Will – under the shade of the old oak tree at the edge of the lawn.

'I'll get the tea and lunch after the others arrive. You two can help me, please.'

'Of course, Mum. But now we have a chance for a quick chat before they come. Have you told Jane and Emily that I'm homosexual?'

She shook her head.

'I thought not. But I'd like them to know, I want everything to be open and honest from now on - so if there's no opportunity today, I leave it to you to tell them. And the other thing is that I've had a military Medical just recently. If they accept me, and I think only my age may be against that, it's possible I'll be sent for training immediately, or more likely within a few months. My superiors in the shop's administration know, I informed them, and they seemed to be very understanding about it, even perhaps approving, and said they would keep my position open for me. So it looks as if things are working out. Ann says – well, you tell Mum, Ann.'

'"Ann says" – oh, what do I say? That I can't bear it, Will going to war, but I'll have to do what women have always had to do, accept an intolerable situation.'

Meg was silent, while she poured tea for them. Then she said 'Well, when Davey went off to war, when he didn't have to, he was even older than you are now, as you know, Will, and I was heart-broken. But – well, I had children and a farm to look after, so – one just had to keep going. Have you heard that song that's so popular now, "We'll meet again"? Vera Lynn, is that her name? And that's what we'll all hope and pray. And Ann, you must come here whenever you want to, whenever you can. So at least you and I can meet again! You know how welcome you'll always be. And now let's be cheerful again! I think I can hear voices – Jane and Emily, oh and Roger -'

'Hullo, all!' Emily greeted them loudly. 'I'm glad we're sitting out in the garden. Makes me sorry we haven't brought the boys, but they're having a good time with friends. How's everyone?'

She and Jane and Roger sat down, and Meg poured them tea. 'And something to eat? There's salad and sandwiches.'

Will had stood up, to shake hands with his brother-in-law. 'So, any news?' They sat down.

Roger: 'All's well, the boys are back to normal, running all over the place. But looks as if the Nazis may be about to attack, that's what they're saying - How is London? Do you think we're prepared? Churchill isn't helping with his "fighting on the beaches" stuff, but maybe you don't agree?'

Meg responded after a moment: 'Yes, I hope we're prepared. It's been so long, waiting and hoping, hoping, hoping that it won't happen - during all these months of "Phoney War". I think we're all worn out by that. But now we have a Prime Minister we can really respect, and even admire - and if *he* can't lead us to victory, who could? That's what *I* think. - But I must call this meeting to order now. Will and Ann have to catch the 2:15 train, Fortune's going to come and pick them up. And we have a couple of important family matters to decide. Who's going to start? Jane, can you tell us about the contents of the bag and what your friend the poetry expert has said?'

'All right. Robin looked carefully at all the material in the bag – which, I think you all know, was given to us by Peter Arnold before he died. There was a novel, but it was mostly illegible, and letters by Dad to Peter and others, and collections of poems by Dad and Peter Arnold. I must say I was quite upset by Robin's opinion. Putting it briefly, he said that Dad's poems – well, he said they were very conventional, mainly sonnets that reminded him of *1914*, he said – you know, the famous set of sonnets by Rupert Brooke – *But* then he said, and as I say I was very surprised, he said that the war-poems by Peter Arnold were, in his words, "startlingly original in every way", powerful and moving, and they should be published as soon as possible – maybe it's too late now, with paper-rationing and all, but certainly *after* the War. Peter Arnold was gassed during the Second Battle of Ypres in 1915 and invalided home, so all his poems are about that battle, of course he didn't experience the

Somme or Passchendaele, but Robin said that didn't matter in the end because what the poems do convey, "unforgettably" he said, is the horror and pity of war – the experience not just of the soldiers but of the citizens of Ypres and the masses of fleeing refugees. So – there you are. I must say that I don't entirely agree with Robin's assessment, but he is a very respected critic and a poet himself.'

Meg sighed. 'Well, what can we say? The expert has spoken. If we agree with him, I think we should send Peter Arnold's poetry to London with Will, and he can take them to a publisher to consider. Do you all agree?'

'I don't really.' Jane smiled wanly. 'But Robin is respected, he's known for his reviews of recent poetry and a book on Great War poetry - so we should start there. About Dad's poems -'

Meg: 'I think we should leave those until later. Keep them somewhere safe, say in the Street Library. You must have a safe, Jane? Yes. And then, after the War – we can discuss what to do with them again. We'll be in a better situation. So that's settled. Any objections? Now I wanted to ask you about the offer from Jane and Roger to - essentially, to exchange houses with me -'

Will: 'But what about Dad's other stuff that you mentioned – letters, and weren't there some sketches?'

Meg was irritated. 'I don't think we should waste time over the letters – there are so many, and not all of them are his – and the sketches, well, they can just be stored with his paintings, they're mainly what he was able to do in the trenches and later used as a basis for his paintings.'

'All right. But the letters may be important, especially Peter Arnold's. What did you think of them, Jane?' and Will turned towards her.

Emily intervened. 'I've looked at the letters too, or should I say I skimmed them. And I agree with Mum and Jane that we don't need to consider them.'

Jane: 'But I didn't say that, Emily. Actually I do think some of them are important, maybe for historians, the ones between Dad and Peter Arnold for instance.'

Meg: 'So, as I said, they can be kept carefully and considered later, when we have more time.'

Will: 'But why not now, when we're together, there may not be another opportunity for a long while. And we're in a war, aren't we? – we don't know what's going to happen.' His voice was rising. 'You know, I glanced at some of them, just randomly, when we were waiting for

what's-her-name, Martha, and you, Mum, while you were in with Peter
– and I have to say -'

Roger spoke. 'What's all this about? I agree with Emily and Jane, they
know what's in those letters, so why should we waste our time now -'

Will: 'All right. What's in those letters, Jane? Why shouldn't we see
them?'

Silence. Then Jane: 'All right, Will, if you insist. I'll tell you. They are
embarrassing. Mum and Emily agree.'

Will: 'So you don't want us to even know about their contents? You
and Mum and Emily want to stop *me* from knowing what's in them?
Because in your opinion they are, what, "embarrassing"?'

Meg suddenly intervened. 'All right, Will. Because they are *disgusting*.
It's because they are, most of them are, love letters from men to men.'

Will: 'And that's *disgusting*? Why? So *I'm* disgusting too -' He stood
up.

Then Roger suddenly stood up, and caught hold of Will's jacket.
They pushed at each other angrily, in silence, until Ann, sitting beside
Will, reached up to pull him back down. Roger looked at Will, his lips
curling. 'Who do you think you are?' he said.

Will smiled angrily. 'Oh, I know who I am. I'm homosexual. How
about you?'

Twenty-six

Returning to London, Ann and Will were again fortunate to find a
compartment to themselves. Fortune had delivered them to the station
in very good time.

After the Family Debate had ended in some confusion, Meg walked
down to the gate with them, upset and inclined to apologise. '–But, Will,
you know Roger's got a short fuse, why antagonise him?'

'*I* antagonise *him!* Come on, Mum, at least say it was mutual. And I
do mean it about those letters – if you don't want them, or can't bear to
read them – well, you remember Peter Arnold wanted *us* to have them,
Ann and me, so if you're going to leave them with Jane, at least ask her to
keep them safe, truly safe, until I can read them properly – I think they'll
have more interest for me than anyone else, but I could be wrong.'

'Anyway, please look after yourselves in London. The news is
troubling, very troubling, as you know. They say to expect heavy air-raids

on London soon. And Ann, I'll be thinking of you, nursing and needing sleep! I hope we can see you here again, very soon. Goodbye – and thank you, Fortune, again.'

'It's a pleasure, Mrs Avery,' he said, and they drove away.

After a moment, Fortune said 'It's good to see you again, Miss. My old friend Jim Sarson told me he happened to meet you at the bridge, near the Clump, where he was fishing, and how you had a chat and looked so pretty, as you always do. And Mr Avery, it's very good to see you and I hope all is going well for you in the Big City.'

'Oh, yes, it is, Mr Fortune. Except for the worry about what Hitler and his Nazis are going to do. But London is well-prepared now, all dark at night – the Black-out - and shelters in Underground Stations, etcetera, and we hear the R.A.F. going over regularly. So if they come, we're ready for them. I hope.'

'Well, that's good to hear, Sir. And Mr Churchill makes a big difference, doesn't he? He's a real leader. Did you hear his last speech? And here we are.'

Ann and Will thanked Fortune and said goodbye, and had a short wait on the platform before the London train arrived.

Once they were seated, 'And what was that all about? The fight with Emily's husband?' Ann asked, as the train jerked into motion.

'Oh, just some bad boyhood memories. I was sent away to a minor public-school, courtesy of my Grandfather's money, as I think you know, and he went to the local grammar-school – mistakenly thought to offer an inferior education to the one I got. More of that dreadful English snobbery. And we used to fight whenever we encountered each other in the holidays. Before that, we'd been good friends. And now he's a good husband and father, and also a rich brother-in-law. Sorry I behaved badly. And I don't think I impressed my two sisters. In fact, I'm sure I didn't.'

Ann turned and kissed him. 'Oh well, you can impress me instead.'

After a few minutes, 'Isn't the human mind strange?' he said. 'A couple of novels have just come into my mind – by Thomas Hardy – *Tess of the D'Urbervilles* and that one, his last one -'

'*Jude the Obscure*. Gloomy, both of them!'

'Yes, so why do they come into my mind now? Maybe *I'm* gloomy. We studied *Tess* in the Fourth Form, and I hated it. She didn't stand a chance, being the creation of such a misanthrope. And then, I should have known better, I came across *Jude* among Dad's books, while you were chatting with Mum last night. *Jude*! And I thought That says something about *him* – Dad, I mean. One scene in that book I can never forget: Jude has to slaughter a pig. Oh, oh, oh, oh. I was devastated. I wonder if Dad was affected by that scene, as much as I was? But why should those books come into my mind now?'

'Because you're depressed. So snap out of it, Sir! Or alternatively, cheer up!'

'Sorry, sorry! No more misery, no more slaughtered milkmaids or pigs. Or bullies – Maybe because of that tiff with bloody Roger, I'm remembering all the bullying at our second-class public-school, by Masters as well as boys – Patriarchal and vindictive, that school - I hated it, and there was the appalling Buttridge - And also it was almost like that at the Royal College of the Arts, that's where I was for three years, I actually won a scholarship - You didn't ask about that, my life and times there, did you? – being told by aged Has-beens that I didn't have enough talent, so I'd better do commercial art. So I left and got a job in the London Shop that I still grace. Which in Buttridge's opinion would be all I am good for. "All you are good for, Boy!"'

'Oh. What can I say, having been spared such extreme atrocities? But instead of your painful reminiscing about the horrors of a privileged English education, you can answer my intelligent queries. Your Father - Davey - the man I once loved, remember? How can *your* Davey and *my* Davey be one and the same? He could be so kind, so considerate – and cheerful. Yet your memory of him seems to be quite different. How come?'

'Oh, he wasn't a harsh or cruel man. He was in fact gentle, and surely we'd agree on that. He could even be ebullient – again we'd agree. But he was often preoccupied, often seemed to be consciously carrying a load of guilt. Or depression. I loved being with him so often, before you first came. When I was a boy of fifteen, sixteen. Before that first bloody war. Did you pick up any of my resentment? Then? After you arrived? You should have, I often projected it at you. But he was infatuated with you – Mum said something like that to me - in an unguarded moment, as they say. And also, yes, he loved Nature, and could write about it beautifully. In articles and even in a few books nobody reads now. His prose was admired by critics – even if nobody wanted to pay him for it. I think he wanted me to follow him and be an artist or writer because he was both. But - Oh, Ann – let's just say that, selfishly, I often felt unfairly ignored by him. And looking back, there was that strange gap between me and the girls. Six years or so, was it? He would often sleep out, in inns or even under hedges – that's how he encountered Peter Arnold, I think. But by then I had got the message that he didn't want me under his feet, or anywhere near him, and so I kept my distance. But Peter Arnold – oh there's much more there, I think, but I don't know if – maybe later -' And Will's voice sank into silence, while he closed his eyes.

The train hurtled on, swaying and whistling loudly as it drummed past minor stations.

'But, Will – I know how complicated it must have been for you, and I'm sorry for any pain I caused you as well. To be honest, or trying to be, as you have been – I just didn't think about you then, except when we were playing games together, you and the girls and me. But that business with Peter Arnold – did he –?'

'Yes, he did, Ann – if I catch your meaning. Might as well talk about it, deal with it. He was always gentle, he never hurt me, but Peter was homosexual and I suppose I knew even then, strange how much we can know even when we don't have the words, or even concepts, to express them - Yes, I knew what he wanted, and sometimes got - he had a small tent he would carry on his back with his camping gear, and sometimes Dad would be in a pub, and Peter – Until Dad found out, or suspected, and then there was a row, I think – and that was the end of my walking with them – because Dad seemed to blame *me*, he wouldn't talk about it, he just – And there was a row between Dad and Peter, a row to end all rows, according to Jane, who told me – I was away at school when it happened – but obviously they patched it up somehow. Until, apparently, the War came and Peter Arnold volunteered immediately and went off and got killed, gassed during the second Battle of Ypres - "Wipers" our soldiers used to call it. And then, next thing, Dad decides to volunteer, even though he was over forty then - but they accepted him, somehow, and a few months later Mum gets that dreadful letter - "Your husband is missing believed dead", she never let me see *that* letter either. So – what more don't you know? You were obviously very busy nursing as a V.A.D., and then marrying your wounded cousin - but of course we knew nothing about that because you had cut yourself off – as you said yourself. Look, even now I don't know everything, but I'll say I'm almost relieved that I can't read those letters in the satchel, I don't even care if Jane and Emily read them all and know more than I ever will – truly, I don't care, it's – well, it's old stuff, and there's a war on! So. I think that's what I think! What else do you want to know? Speak now or evermore be silent!'

Ann: 'Well, all right. My story. You asked for it, and you know it. It's a simple story, well known, often repeated. Young girl is infatuated with older man. Until he tires of her – But he did kiss me, once – under the old apple-tree near the Cottage. He was always kind to me, and we always enjoyed walking together, loving Nature, the Outdoors. So I would definitely call it love, on both sides. Certainly there was no anger or bad feelings. Yes, but now I am thinking more about your Mother – how she put up with me -'

'Oh, now - I have a different opinion. You helped keep their marriage going. She saw you were no real danger, in fact you endorsed and preserved their marriage. The girls adored you, and you occupied them positively, and that gave Mum more freedom – She was actually running the farm, Dad didn't do much - He said, I heard him, "Your father gave *you* this farm, so you're in charge!" – But he did contribute to it financially as well as he could. While he was with us. But he left us for five or six years, as I said - He just wasn't there – Now, I think he was with Peter Arnold, or other men, maybe even living in a sort of commune, a group of artists, who knows? And we just didn't talk about him, just picked up that Mum didn't want to talk about him. She said to me "*You're* the man of the house now."

'And Mum and I – we were so happy in those years. And then, one day, he was there – he was back, and whatever was said between him and Mum, life just changed shape and moved on for me, and that's when - Oh, there's always much more to be said, to be understood, isn't there? And I think we're coming into London.'

They walked from the station through streets lapsing into twilight.

'I love London' he said suddenly. 'The Nazis can never destroy it. Never, never. Only we can.'

But that night the Nazis tried. Bombs fell. Buildings collapsed. Parts of the City burned. Blitz. The Battle of Britain was beginning.

Dear Will and Ann,

SURPRISE! Bet you never expected to get a letter from me - Emily!! Wonders will never cease, as Roger often says (one of his father's sayings)!

I'm writing because Mum asked me to write to you two. I tried to phone but no answer! After you left us on Sunday, Mum had a fall!!! It was in the kitchen in the cotage, near the Aga in the kitchen. Roger and me had gone home by then (also Jane, we gave her a lift to the libary), so we didn't know till the next morning, Fortune phoned us. She had tripped in the kitchen over Skippy (she didn't see him, she didn't know he was behind her!), she banged her head, and fainted, but after a while she crawled to the phone and got through to Fortune and he came straghtaway and drove her to the hospital.

You musn't worry!! She's ALL RIGHT, she said I must tell you that. And that you musn't think about coming, she'll be out of hospital tomorrow and then I'll be looking after her, in the cottage. Roger and me and the Boys have moved into the cottage now (we would have moved here a bit later, we and Mum had decided to swop our houses during the War, at least, I think you know that, so we can help her, the Boys love to help feeding the animals and I'll be able to do the housekeeping and make sure she eats right. Then we won't have to worry about her, and about the cotage too, as I say the Boys will enjoy helping me look after all the animals and feeding the hens (they are very excited, the Boys I mean), and of course me and Roger will be in charge.

That seems to be the best solution, I hope you will agree. And after Mum is back tomorrow (Fortune will bring her, he said) we will go through her things with her when she feels up to it and pack what she wants for when she can move into our house in Street where she'll be close to evrything (but no hurry of course, she can take as long as she likes, and when she feels ready she says she'll say so).

Jane agrees with us that this arrangement is for the best! So I hope you will think so too!

Please look after yourselves in London, everyone seems to think that the Nazi invasion is coming soon! (If so, we hope they won't march through

*Street on their way to London!) You already have bombing and air-raids,
we know, so please be very careful!!!!*

Lots of love from all of us – and Skippy! Look after yourselves!

Your loving Sister,
Emily

Twenty-seven

Ann and Will met for supper in the Crown and Sceptre, a pub just round
the corner from the Hospital and not far from Will's big Department-
store. 'The Crown is for you, obviously, my Queen', he had said, 'and I
must be the Sceptre, which symbolises my male dominance of course.'
Preceding him through the doorway, she had smiled easily, sceptical but
complaisant; and thinking that the pub, conveniently close to Will's flat,
had quickly become their almost-daily meeting-place, where they would
eat a meal together, as his supper and her breakfast.

Increasingly destructive air-raids had not damaged their area of
London yet; but on August the 15th an urgent siren made everyone in
the pub very nervous, and that night Croydon was attacked. The long-
feared Blitz was beginning.

Will had already spent a few sleepless nights in the Underground
Station near his flat, in response to the wail of sirens; while Ann and her
fellow-nurses were struggling to keep the hospital running as smoothly
as possible, watchfully supporting the doctors and other necessary
medical staff.

In the pub, there was a tendency to whisper amongst those regulars
still brave or foolhardy enough to sit at the bar with their pints of Bitter
and plates of Scotch pie or fish-and-chips, engaging the gruff Publican in
nervous badinage.

Will led the way to a table in a gloomy corner (what with the Black-
out and reduced lighting, they would all be blind before long, from
prolonged eye-strain, he had asseverated). 'Well, at least we can sit and
exchange news of the day before you have to go back to the Hospital,'
he would say, 'and tomorrow I have to go back to the unending struggle
to keep the shop going – of course, suppliers are reluctant to supply in
present circumstances. So much work now to keep the shop running
properly! We had a visitation this afternoon from a delegation of Senior

Managers – "Chin up, chin up!' – but they did give some encouragement and assurance, and even approval, saying we should feel free to stay overnight in the shop if things get really bad, and that there will be camp-beds available in the Haberdashery Department!'

Ann laughed shortly, then sighed, out of sheer weariness. 'Oh. At least maybe I can look forward to day-duty after this weekend. I'm *exhausted*. Didn't get much sleep, the streets seemed to be full of roaring vehicles and the air seemed to be full of a screeching siren. But - How long can we take this, do you think, Will? How can it be August already - where did the Spring go? And soon Summer will be gone. But all the months of apprehension, they just go *on and on* – always half an ear or eye open for explosions, the distant whine of German 'planes, hoping that the Barrage Balloons will keep them away – and in the – Oh, I don't know what I was going to say. I'm just too tired to think. Already the nursing's nearly as bad, nearly as exhausting, as during the First War. But, Will, how long do you think we, you and I and all the people in London and other cities – how long can we possibly take it?'

'As long as we have to. Churchill says we'll fight on the beaches etcetera etcetera – that we have "nothing to offer but blood, tears and sweat", but of course he's right, and he knows how to say it effectively and memorably – that we just have to survive, at whatever cost. At least that's better than the alternative. Which reminds me – I've passed my Medical, and they wanted to know which Service I'd prefer – though of course if I say the R.A.F., which I did, they're likely to put me into the Navy.'

'Oh, and I've had a communication too – from your Mother.'

'Before you tell me about that, Ann – I forgot to say that I telephoned her last night, and actually got through on quite a good line. She says she's feeling fine now – "Hitler can't kill off this old girl", though of course her fall had nothing at all to do with the Fuhrer. And she said that Roger has accepted my apology.'

'Your apology? When did you -?'

'I didn't, of course. And anyway, it's such a long time ago that I'm surprised anyone remembers or cares. But oh - you know, Mum also mentioned Sarson, and Dunkirk. *Dunkirk* - You and me, Ann, we hardly talked about Dunkirk, did we? Hardly even mentioned it – Of course we knew it was a disaster, with our Army defeated by the Germans, who were getting control of France and would be able to invade England from there – it seemed like the beginning of the end, it seemed almost that we were doomed, and that can still happen of course. But the miraculous evacuation of the British Army from the beaches of Dunkirk under Nazi bombing, in April or June wasn't it? when the Nazis were invading and conquering France. That really seemed like a miracle, didn't it? Dunkirk. We had so many other things to do and think about at that time, *all the time*, you and me and so many others. But Dunkirk - when many English boats, including little fishing-boats from the Channel ports, risked everything to save so many soldiers who were being slaughtered on Dunkirk beaches – it still does seem like a miracle. And in one of those little boats, Mum said, was a friend of an old friend of Mum's, Sarson - the man, you remember, you told me you met when you walked to the Clumps. Mum said they sailed across the Channel at least three times, Sarson and his friend - Before the War they used to go ocean-fishing together, and so they sailed across the Channel to Dunkirk in the friend's fishing-boat and rescued as many soldiers off the beach as they could, until – well, Mum says, the boat just disappeared, probably bombed by a German 'plane. She and Fortune have been very upset about it ever since, she said, because Sarson was a good friend of theirs, and well-known and popular in Street. What they did, those two old men and other men like them, what they achieved, was just like Churchill's "We will fight on the beaches, we will *never* surrender", and so they helped to turn a British disaster into a sort of triumph! Didn't they? That's what I think. And maybe, if the Germans don't invade and defeat us, what those men, even old men like Sarson, what they did will be a reason, maybe even the main reason, who knows? So the courage of Sarson and other old men like him could help us defeat Hitler in the end? What do you think? Another of my crazy ideas? But I'm sorry I forgot to mention all this before, Ann – what Mum said. Seems we have so many other things to think about, worry about, all the time. And now, Ann – I said I wanted to talk to you about my Mother. I think you don't really know much about her.'

'Don't -? How can you possibly say that? Do you actually think I know hardly anything about her, after so long? And you must admit, she's been very good to me – kind, generous, forgiving, in spite of my failures in the past. Oh, Will. Let's not talk about family relations and family problems at a time like this. I'm just too tired. Really.'

'But if not now – when? Ann, I know you're tired, I know I am too. And fearful. Any moment the siren might start up again and we'll have to run for the Underground. You're going to a night of nursing, and I hate to think of how hard that will be, *is,* at this time. I think often of all the nurses, truly I do, and especially of the one I love so much. Can I kiss her?'

'Oh, Will. But don't dare to stain my uniform, I can't take any more of Matron's sarcasm. And now that I look at you – when did you last shave, Mister? No, *I'll* kiss *you*' and she did.

He leant back smiling, with eyes closed, but after a few moments stood up – 'I'll just be going back to my office for a final look at accounts and orders. And then I'll get my night's sleep – I hope. Oh, don't listen – I'm just repeating myself again – I'm like you, so tired that I'm stupid. Do you know, do you ever have time to *think*, that Christmas is not far off! *Next* Christmas. So start planning! Welcome, Jesus, to the world your Father has created.'

'*Will!* Oh, that's – you *can't -*' Ann was shocked by his levity. But why? she asked herself.

'Yes, I can. I must. And that letter from Emily – did you realise that we can't spend even one night in the Cottage now? But at least Mum will be all right. Of course. And look, I've finished my fish-and-chips and I need another pint. While I see to my needs – which include a trip to the loo – you finish your supper, and I promise I won't take longer than fifteen minutes to say my say, after which I'll escort you to the Hospital on my way home. As usual. Agreed?'

Ann sighed. 'All right. But you have to keep to your script – no more speechifying – *You* may think your speeches are as good as Mr Churchill's but I - '

He raised his eyebrows, smiled briefly. A warm, weary smile. 'Oh, and I forgot, Ann: I love you.'

When he returned, with his second Bitter, and threw himself back into his chair, Ann said 'Sorry, Mister, now *I* have an appointment, mainly to wash my face and hands. Nurses have to have higher standards of cleanliness than mere passing males. "Be back in a tick", is that what the English say? Or "in a jiffy"?'

When she came back, he said 'While you were away I had a sudden thought: "Cox and Box".'

'What's that? Or - Who are they?'

'Of course you wouldn't know, but maybe you should! Gilbert and Sullivan – they wrote a series of rather silly late-Victorian operettas, which all public-schools performed regularly, mine certainly did - I was a Pirate of Penzance! do you know that one? – But the first one was about two men who alternated in sleeping, like us, in one bed, one of them during the day and the other one through the night – And that's all I remember about "Cox and Box", so let's get on' and he looked at his watch. 'I have ten minutes to make my case, and you have five for comment or rebuttal. Here we go. Topic number one: My Mother. Ann – she is *not* a Saint. But, maybe, you say, not a Sinner like the rest of us. Think: has she always been positive, straightforward?'

'Yes.'

'Remember, I have a much longer experience of her than you have. And of my Father. And of their marriage and parenting. Why did he go away for what, five years or more? I was at my ghastly public-school later, but Jane – who, by the way, has always been much more observant and communicative than Emily – told me about their huge, *violent* rows – and she even voiced some sympathy for him. What was the reason for that battle? – Because it *was* a battle, a war to end all wars, according to Jane's account. I can only speculate that Peter Arnold was somehow involved. Because, according to Jane's account, he was very close to Dad then – and probably, I speculate, encouraging him to write poetry – *Write, write, write, Davey!* – maybe recognising that Dad's poems weren't very good, but, knowing his prose, hopeful of radical improvement. All right, he seems to have been wrong – or partially wrong – and, as posterity may show, the true war-poet, maybe the *great* war-poet, is Peter Arnold. I think Dad recognised that, and after Peter was gassed on the Western Front and nearly died, he decided that he had to try to - had to take Peter's place as it were - I wonder if this makes sense? - he had to try to *replace* Peter. So he volunteered, was accepted, and died on the battlefield not very long afterwards – having sent his poems to Mum for safekeeping.'

'Will. Please - I'll have to go very soon – I mustn't be late.'

'Yes, I know. Anyway, I'm almost finished. Did you notice that Mum didn't want us even to *see* Dad's poems or letters? And of course she never really wanted any of us children to be close to Dad, when he came back – that was obvious – even Emily said that. Remember, Mum was an only child, and had inherited all that her father had to leave, especially the Farm. She was used to having total control. She was used to running the show. And now I'm nearly finished. Ann, I had to say all this. For my own sake, not Mum's, of course – she will be fine – Emily and Roger are there for her, in total support, and she will use Crab-apple Farm as her retirement insurance. But, Ann – I'm not saying Mum is a villain – Some people even dare, you know, *still* - to say or think that Hitler only wanted, for his people, what the Allies, at the end of the First War, took for themselves in the Treaty of Versailles. Maybe your pacifist friend would concur? So could there be any truth in that? Is evil only on one side? Or are we all evil, all of us, and *all* need to be kept in line? And sometimes I think What does any of it matter? We'll be dead soon, and all of us will be dead in a hundred years – *all of us.* If not in the War, in this Blitz, as they're calling it - just expiring as our bodies wear out. Yes, all right, time's up! Time, gentlemen, please! Thank you for listening to my harangue, Ann. Now back to your Hospital.'

Again the lights flickered. The Publican looked worried. Will put their two empty glasses in front of him and said cheerfully, reaching for his gas-mask, 'Thank you, Tom. Have a good night!'

Twenty-eight

Ann and Will meet in the Crown and Sceptre during the evening of Sunday 18th August: her breakfast, his supper; again. Their conversation is desultory. He orders a pint of Bitter with Fish-and-chips, she asks for Water with Toad-in-the-hole.

'I was just thinking, Will, how long is it since we were last at Crab-apple Cottage? Must be several months – many months. We just go on and on with our lives here from day to day, night to night. Who would have guessed that war could become so routine?'

'Oh, not exactly routine, my dear Ann! There seems to be always more to do and think about – just to survive and do all the necessary things, routine or not. Checking the Black-out every night, making sure you have your gas-mask with you, spending all those dreadful nights in the Underground, more and more often – so noisy and uncomfortable, though I know we're supposed to enjoy the comradeship and singsongs etcetera – thank goodness there hasn't been too much of that so far. But more opportunities to come, I fear, with the help of Herr Hitler. And then we have our jobs to do.'

'But what about that possibility of peace you talked about – was it a year ago? When Herr Hitler offered us a peace plan and we rejected it – or Herr Churchill did?'

'But that's very old news now, Ann! And of course the Germans would have wanted all of our colonies etcetera etcetera as payment for their great generosity. But who knows? Churchill was the one who stopped that peace possibility in its tracks, everyone thinks that – and a lot of people, including me, think he was right. But, as I say, who knows? Maybe the answer depends on what happens in the future – when, like the poor inhabitants of France, we have to endure invasion or severe attack? And who can predict our future – apart from that over-confident so-called-war-monger Winston Churchill? And what about your pacifist friend, the one who gave a talk in Street, the one who was on your ship coming over from America? I wonder what *she* thinks now? – now that the Nazi hordes are about to invade us? Am I repeating myself? Sorry, Ann – another of my diatribes, and I hope I didn't raise my voice too much – I see Tom looking at me - and' in a whisper 'a couple of silent imbibers.'

'Well, all right, let me change the subject.' Ann smiled apologetically towards customers seated at nearby tables, and spoke quietly. 'Don't you think the Royal Family are setting all of us such a good example? The little Princesses – they make me remember Jane and Emily as little girls, all that we did together in the distant past. And the King and Queen. So very brave. And of course Mr Churchill and his speeches, also very inspiring – when he's not away on some secret journey. But I was thinking how I seem to have *totally* lost connection, in the last few months, with my previous life, or lives – in Canada, obviously, but even here. And as I was saying, even with your Mother, your sisters, your nephews – and Crab-apple Cottage, and Skippy and the other animals. Am I just being sentimental?'

'Yes, maybe. But there's a remedy for that. Let's 'phone Mum and say we'd like to come next weekend – or as soon as possible – as soon as the Hospital can spare you. I think most weekends would still be fine for me. I can arrange for some of the others to look after things in the Shop for a short while, if there's no crisis. And we could stay in Street's *Royal Hotel.* That shouldn't break the bank. I think the trains are running – or most of them.'

'All right - I'll try to get through to one of them. After I get back to the flat tomorrow morning, I'll try to get through to Meg. Before I go to sleep. Or *hope* to sleep. Oh, how tired and stupid I feel! But I should warn you, too, that the Hospital may object – Matron has been on the warpath about Standards again, and the need to keep on keeping on.'

'But, Ann – I woke up last night, there were some distant explosions, and while I was lying there, before I got to sleep again, I thought Why are you still always on Night-duty? – you said you'd ask the Matron for Days for at least some of the time.'

'Yes, well I didn't. If I'm on Days - and remember we're short-staffed now - one of the others has to take my place on Nights – and I know that several of them have small children who they worry about more and more, as the Luftwaffe night-raids become more and more frequent and destructive. So – it's a struggle for all of us, but much worse for them than for me. At least we don't have children, Will. And maybe that's a blessing as things are?'

'I think we're all struggling, Ann. Yesterday an elderly man came into the shop when I was helping in the Foods section and he wanted to buy cat-food, and after he'd gone Janet said "It's not for a cat - I know his wife, she's very old and bed-ridden and he has to cope somehow, and they probably have no money, or family - I tried to talk to him about his situation, but he wouldn't, he has his pride". And there are so many like him, elderly men and women mainly, and all the poor people, struggling, one knows that – but how can we help them? – But we're now at least setting out some food and fruit near the main entrance of the Shop, for people to take if they need it. And then there's rationing, and shortages of more and more items – sometimes even "essential" items.'

'In the Hospital we're also beginning to run short of things – equipment, medication. But some *is* coming now, mainly from American charities. There were two difficult births last night, and I had to help – I'll be a midwife yet! But some of the hardest cases, as I was telling you, are survivors of that bombing in the West, was it Cardiff? – their terrible terrible wounds - and some of those people are incredibly brave, even the children. All of us nurses were very upset a few nights ago when one child, who we all thought was likely to pull through, suddenly died – just died, as if he'd decided it really wasn't worth living any more. And I guess we were all asking ourselves "Was it *my* fault?"'

'Well, we both have our jobs to do. What more is there to say? We must just survive.'

'Yes, and it's almost time for me to get myself to the Hospital, Will – and tomorrow I'll need a real good sleep, so I hope the Luftwaffe will co-operate. And I think it's raining.'

'But before we go, Ann - Don't I deserve a kiss after my day of shopworn toil? Well, actually I want more than a quiet half-concealed kiss this time. I want more, more, *more.*' And he stood up abruptly, nearly knocking the small table over. Ann caught his empty beer-mug before it fell. Then she stood up too, nervously, and Will embraced her ostentatiously.

'Pay attention, everybody!' His voice was again loud, forceful. All the nearby customers in the pub, sitting at the bar or around small tables, stopped talking, and looked at him. The publican, Tom, stopped wiping glasses.

'My name is William and this is Ann. We are your neighbours' Will said, loudly. And then stopped abruptly.

A young man who had been sitting alone at the nearest table jumped up, and came forward to stand beside Will. 'Yes,' he said loudly, 'and we are *your* neighbours, William. My name is Trevor. And I apologise for listening-in to some of your conversations, but I feel I really know you both by now. Ann and William. You are in love. Anyone can see that! And so by the authority of this old noble beer-infested London pub, I declare you married, well and truly *married*. And now – kiss each other!'

So they did. To loud applause.

And after that, Will thanked Trevor, and his uncle, Tom the Publican; and then, arm in arm, Will and Ann walked round the pub, thanking all present for their nuptials; and then Tom called out jokingly 'Time, gentlemen – and ladies – please! Drink up, now – the wedding's over, and I declare that life will continue!' And finally, arm in arm, dangling their gas-masks, Will and Ann set off.

On their way to the hospital, she suddenly giggled, stopped, and leant against a wall. 'Now, if I'm ever late, and Matron bellows at me, I will look her in the eye and say – what will I say? That I am *Mrs William Avery*, I am a *Married Woman* and I expect more respect than I have yet received.' She giggled again. 'You too, dearest Husband, whenever I have something to say - And the first thing is: Don't try to fool me in the future, Sir! Next time we get married, I want a *real* Minister, not the Publican's son, and I want a *real* marriage service, with a certified Priest, in a Church. - Yes I know, I'm a bit, what is it you say, "tiddly"? on cider! But this is wartime and who knows what's going to happen to us all? So I forgive you, dear Will – if you will give me another kiss, and lead me safely to the Hospital. And don't worry – I'll sober-up quickly, once I see Matron's glare, and anyway the other Nurses would cover for me if necessary. Also, I'm over forty – so, Mister, now *you* can *fuck off*.'

Twenty-nine

Will: 'It's the Blitzkrieg, it's the endless Battle for Britain. At last, it's here. France is conquered and occupied. Now they'll attack us and try to bomb us into submission and then invade. Last night was Hell – you must have realized that in the Hospital, however busy you all were – and I know you must have been. Oh, Ann. What is there to say?'

'Yes. Total exhaustion. We never stopped, it was one ambulance after another. But – I do have something to tell you. Two things, maybe, but I'll start with just one. Remember that pacifist woman I told you about? Soon after I met you? Well – of course I had no idea she and her husband are living in one of those big apartments along the road, not very far from us – But then, suddenly, there she was, on a gurney, with her face covered in blood, and groaning – so we had to clean her up and get her into a bed. Then the husband suddenly appeared, with blood and dust all over him. He was gabbling, saying there had been an air-raid and a bomb had been dropped onto the block of flats next-door to theirs – and the two of them, he and his wife, had been in their cellar before that, after hearing the siren, and then, when the "All Clear" came, he said, they were just going upstairs to dress - apparently she was to give a talk, he said that several times - when there was a huge explosion, in the building right next-door, I guess a delayed-action bomb or maybe a gas-leak, so they were rushing back down the stairs, when she tripped and fell and knocked herself out, I think she must have been quite badly concussed, and then he ran out into the street calling for help, and – you won't believe this! the taxi they had ordered was actually there, just arrived, and the Cabbie immediately helped, carrying her to the taxi, and then driving them to the Hospital – "And he wouldn't even let me pay him!" the husband said – Oh, those London cabbies, they are amazing, aren't they! Anyway, I'm telling you all this because I was of course worried about them, so I spoke to him, and he actually remembered me. He told me he'd stay with her through the rest of the night, and of course I had a lot of other patients to see to, apart from the new ones. But when I managed to find time to check up on them later, they were gone – she was sent to the Emerg, I heard later. But, and this was a surprise, he had left an envelope containing a typed article, apparently the one she would have been presenting, and scrawled on it was this, "For the Nurse who was a VAD". Look, here it is. It's entitled "*Sursum Corda*" – what's that actually mean? It's Latin, isn't it?'

'Yes. It means "Lift up your hearts". Strange title for an article about the War, don't you think? I'd like to read it, so hand it over, Mrs Avery. And now *my* latest news, if you're interested? Yes? Well, to my surprise I got a summons from our company's Administrative Committee which entailed being picked up by a rather smart Rolls-Royce and driven to Company Headquarters in the West End. Why? you ask, bewildered. To cut a long story short, I was favoured with an interview presided over by the Founder himself – he's ancient, at least ninety, but apparently *compos mentis*, and some members of the Board of Governance were in attendance. No doubt others had more important matters to attend to, especially with the bombing last night. But – Well, briefly: this is what I experienced. His Mightiness announced, "Mr Avery, we have heard very good things about your administration of our Oxford Street shop, so we know that you are not only capable but also humane, with very high approval from your staff and customers, so we are offering you promotion to Supervisor, and also Membership of the Board, congratulations, Mr Avery.'" Will paused.

'Oh, and *my* congratulations too, Mr Avery.'

'Thank you.' He bowed. '*But*. But that isn't quite the end of my story. In reply I said, I felt I *had* to say, "I intended to tell you, Sir, as soon as it was official, that I have applied for acceptance into the Royal Air Force." And then what happened? I expected silence, or disapproving looks maybe – but no, the Old Boy burst into smiles, congratulated me fervently – actually leaned over the table to shake my hand - and then said "We will hold your position for you while you are serving your King and Country, young man. You are demonstrating what we should all demonstrate: a deep love for England and for its capital, our beloved London.' -"*Young man!!*" But then I *am* only half his age – Anyway, he went on "You are a credit to our Company! And the Company's very best wishes will go with you." Now, can you beat that?'

'Maybe I can, darling Spouse. Exhausted as she is, your Wife will rise to the challenge. – Oh, Will, I do love you! And I do congratulate you. You deserve all that praise. - But what is *my* story? I have been holding it back for a suitable moment, and now it can follow *your* big moment. I will be brief, my darling, as you were in narrating your story. You remember my Matron, who I have been complaining about? Well, she turns out to have a heart of gold! Honestly! She came up behind me while I was bed-making a few nights ago and I thought Oh no, what have I done *now*? Well, she actually smiled at me, which must have damaged her facial-muscles – oh, I'm being mean again! Then she said "Nurse, I have noticed that you seem to love tending to children and young people, and that they respond very well indeed to your care. So I have decided to submit a recommendation that, if you are agreeable, you should be given the opportunity of advanced training in that area. *Are* you agreeable?' Well, how could I dare to say No? So I didn't. I smiled sweetly and thanked her.

And why am I so deferential to her? I asked myself that, once again, while I was still smiling my gratitude. Answer: She is probably only a few years older than me, but she is a *trained registered-nurse* and I have been, *am,* a mere V.A.D., whose role is to serve doctors and *real* nurses – I learned that during the First War. I guess I could have qualified as a Nurse later, in Canada, but I always saw myself as primarily serving and supporting my cousin, as if I was unofficially married to him, I mean before I *was* married to him. And he did insist that I should control and use his money, which included an inheritance from his mother. So you might say I am like Mr Fortune: capable, sometimes indispensable, even mildly wealthy, but, alas, lower-class? Well, maybe no longer. The transformation can't be immediate, but it will happen – Matron said "soon", and I'm looking forward to it – working with children – and becoming a proper, official Nurse.'

'So. There it is, and well-deserved, long-deserved. Congratulations, my dear Wife. Soon you won't want me, you'll replace me with the patter of little adopted feet, while you climb ever upwards towards the ultimate rapture of Matronhood. And become that impossible person, a Canadian Matron with a Heart of Gold. Meanwhile, let us kiss, and kiss again, with unabated joy.'

'Oh, Will, you *are* a fool, and I love you for it, even if your mother and sisters don't. But, mentioning Mr Fortune makes me feel very guilty, and you should feel guilty too. Because we didn't even think, I know *I* didn't, when we last saw him, to express condolence for the loss of his friend Sarson, was that his name, during the Dunkirk evacuation. And of course Mr Fortune didn't say anything. Or did all that happen *after* we were there? And how is it that *he* survived? Oh, but of course he wasn't - You know - I think I'm totally confused – about everything. Are we all just zombies now? How can we carry on? Surely this *has* to end? '

They leaned towards each other and he managed to kiss her closed eyes, once, while she sighed and shivered.

Thirty

Ann was awakened by loud explosions. The whole house seemed to groan and shiver. She heard the siren's wail – from the Docks, or were they bombing the West End now? – Hard to tell the direction from where I am, but looks as if the Battle for Britain that they've been prophesying may actually be starting – I think maybe I'm hearing not just explosions but the whine of 'planes. What's today? Wednesday 21st August, 1940. Maybe I should get up, and get myself down into the cellar – but, honestly, I hate being in the cellar, where you can't know what is happening, and the air is fetid – I'd rather be up here and take my chances. I hope Will is safe, I hope he -

When Will gets back to the flat, in mid-afternoon, Ann is fast asleep. He looks down at her face, studying in silence its gentle curves – lips, cheeks, eyebrows, ears, hair – and listens to the soft sound of her breathing. The competing sounds of siren and distant explosions are weakening.

He sits down at the small desk beside the window, and draws a folder out of the leather case he has been carrying under his right arm. Soon a fragile near-silence takes control.

He has started a letter to Ann in his office, and now continues it, writing swiftly with his fountain-pen.

My dearest Ann, this is a love-letter, but also I must record some other thoughts in case it becomes impossible for me to continue writing after this. I LOVE YOU – never forget that, please. You have, as they say, changed my life, and very very much for the better. For the BEST. If I believed in God, I would thank him and thank him again and again for bringing you here from Canada at this dangerous time. In a way (we talked about this, and we feel the same way) it is good that your Father's time ended before this War really got under way.

I STARTED THIS LETTER IN MY OFFICE and now maybe I will finish it (if I can keep my eyes open long enough!). It's still raining out there, I think, a gentle steady soundless rain – I got quite wet coming home. The whole city seems quiet at the moment, just breathing gently again – no air-raids, no sirens, no bombs falling. But for how long?

You need to sleep during the day, and I need to sleep at night – it's called team-work! (Or Cox and Box – sorry!) So now you are sleeping deeply and gently near me – you need that sleep, you must have it. I am home early, weary, so weary, after struggling with orders and accounts, etcetera (many shortages now – rationing very necessary), but I'm still much too restless to lie down yet - and strangely the sounds of war have really diminished. There is so much I want to tell you, and I know I can't do it all here and now – maybe, if we both survive this second world war, I'll be able to tell you everything – or maybe not! But I'll make the effort.

It starts, my part of the story, with being virtually banished from my Father's company, and realising that Peter Arnold was more important to him than I was. Why? That's what puzzled me, and maybe I still don't know fully. Of course they were both wanderers, loved nothing more than walking through the English countryside, and painting it, and writing about it, and sleeping under hedges. I didn't fit into that picture. And you didn't, really, either – but you are a woman and so exempt from sleeping under hedges - and Dad enjoyed falling in love with you, and having the great pleasure of your company (You can see that in some ways I am my Father's son!). But THERE WAS MORE TO IT with Dad and Peter, their close relationship, I realised. And one day, before they really turned against me, I heard them talking quietly (I was near them, behind a hedge, listening - as in that Jane Austen novel you admire so much!). And what I heard, or thought I heard -

Well, here comes some History first. At the end of the Great War (Eleventh hour of the Eleventh day of the Eleventh month! How we loved rolling that off our tongues!) there was a Conference to decide how the Victors would humiliate the Victim by grabbing as much of his territory as they could. This was known as the TREATY OF VERSAILLES – and it set up a situation that led directly to this War. (Few Historians, I think, would accept that – but how can one avoid it?)

I should also point out, in a spirit of inappropriate playfulness, how the early months that we've been living through of THIS Great War (I've heard them called THE PHONEY WAR recently) balance the period after THAT Great War when, although fighting had ceased in November 1918, there was a period, before the Treaty of Versailles, of similar length to our Phoney War; when apparently nothing much was happening (it was called THE ARMISTICE). A joke at our expense by the Cosmos? Perhaps. But now the joke is ending, may already have ended. Even as I am writing these words. And who knows how many many MANY of us will be destroyed, will be dead or horribly wounded, by the end of THIS Great War? (Many have died already, yes I know, but not so many right here yet, and not yet our friends and relatives, and not yet so many fellow-citizens in our green and pleasant land.) And how many changes, positive but mainly negative, like those ordained by the Great War, lie in wait for us?

Oh, Ann. You were stirring, and I was tempted to touch you, kiss you, wake you up. Talk to you. But you need your sleep, as you have said and as I certainly know - so I didn't. Later, yes -

Back to my story, which is also, I think, more than just my story.

See what you think! You of course know nothing of my forebears – my maternal grandfather, especially. I have little memory of him. Grey hair, wrinkles, a lordly presence. Yes, that's it: lordly. Though he was actually a servant of the local aristocracy – He was also educated and ambitious, beyond his companions and contemporaries, with enough intelligence and determination to advance towards upper-class status. (Poor Fortune, of course, lacks that talent and ambition – goodness of heart doesn't qualify.) I've already mentioned the Versailles Conference of 1919 which was tasked with tidying up after the Great War. The "Big Four" leaders who dominated that forum were Woodrow Wilson of the U.S.A., David Lloyd George (Gt Britain), Georges Clemenceau (France) and Vittorio Orlando (Italy). Tasked with reorganising Europe for a peaceful future, they set about seizing what territory they could and quarrelled over ownership of the rest. A distasteful and baleful spectacle. Hardly predictive of a Peaceful Future! And what did my Grandfather have to do with it? Through his connection with the Conservative Party and Lloyd George, he became a power behind their Conference throne, and (cutting a long story very short) was well-rewarded for his political manipulations, in London as well as Paris. One of the things he did with that acquired money and status was to buy property in and near Street (of course he already owned Crab-apple Farm). BUT THAT WAS NOT ENOUGH!!! So, with his excellent political connections, he became, for a while, an unchallengeable power in this part of the Kingdom. A local Lord of the Manor, no less. BUT he had SECRETS.

Ann, I fear this is all very boring for you. However it is significant for my family, for me. And it is HISTORY. So, briefly. My Mother, as the only legitimate descendant, inherited Crab-apple Farm, which in those days was productive and lucrative. But I'm sorry to say that my Grandfather had no respect for rules or moral standards. Peter Arnold was an illegitimate son of his – he was my Uncle, in fact (did you guess that?) - who became my Father's closest friend and confidant. By chance or by design? I think my Mother had some inkling of that situation – which probably explains, at least in part, her intransigence over Dad's and Peter's letters. She may also know (I'm sure she does) that the Fortune family have long had a close connection with my Grandfather, who is now deceased – a typically-English relationship of lower-class subservience and upper-class arrogance.

Well, I mustn't go on about my family history – what I have gleaned of it. Or guessed about it. In fact, if you find all this stuff sad and destructive, Ann – I agree! The only justification I can find for this War is that it might finally sweep away much of the Bad Stuff! Why can't we start again? As a society of respected equals. You'll say that is impracticable – it would be COMMUNISM! But surely we must try to know and understand as much as possible about our society, and about who we are, as human-beings, animals who slaughter each other and other animals - animals who will eventually destroy the whole planet and all its inhabitants. ('There he goes!' you're thinking.) Maybe we can try to reduce the harm we do? If that's all we can do, at least let's try to do that. What do you think? I know we'll discuss all this. And you'll say "Will, Will, Will, Will! You have more Sensibility than Sense. You're talking nonsense again" – yet again.

But there's more, Ann! Who was my Father? Where did he come from? Was he a stranger from the North (like Hardy's Mayor of Casterbridge)? And was my Mother "desperate", as they used to say, for a husband? Anyway, they married. He was a highly-educated "literary" man, who loved the countryside, and writing, but not the hard work of running a farm. So then this happened: He committed suicide, or was murdered, on the Western Front, during the Great War, on instructions that probably came from my wealthy and powerful Grandfather, his Father-in-law. You gasp (or so I imagine) - if you're paying attention! Can you believe what I have just written? Do I believe it? Does it even make sense? I gasped when I saw Peter talking quietly to Dad not long before he set off for the Western Front. Surely Peter was giving him a warning? Which Dad just ignored, when he volunteered and became a soldier on the Western Front after Peter was badly wounded? Far-fetched? But how can I ever know the truth now? What ACTUALLY HAPPENED? Where is the evidence? And who am I, to have any hope of discovering the Truth – am I a Historian? No, I'm a Shop-keeper. And does it MATTER now, any of it?

But Ann, there's one more shocking truth to tell about Dad and Peter: they were friends who grew very close to each other, during the five years Dad was absent from his wife and son before the Great War (Where were they? In a commune is my favourite conjecture, which is probably a-historical - maybe they went abroad?). Anyway, to condense this account now, I think he rejected me, his son, for Peter, his friend or lover – and when Peter volunteered to fight in the War (why?), and was badly wounded, Dad decided to replace him as a soldier. Can any of this be true? Does it make any sense? What do you think? 'Speculative nonsense!!' And if Peter truly was Mum's half-brother -? That might explain - Oh, a crazy thought! Madness! 'Forget it all, Will!!!!!' Yes.

I need to stop, dear Ann. And return to sanity. We will talk about such matters. If you wish to. And you can tell me if you think me crazy. But meanwhile - Time, gentlemen, please! And I need my sleep too – not as much as you need yours, of course, but enough to enable me to keep my little corner of London's Commerce functioning, however many bombs fall on us. England demands no less! So here endeth.

Your loving lover, Will, on Wednesday 21st August, 1940

P.S. Ann, I'm really a story-teller, I think. Like my Father! And a good story beats a historical fact any day – in fact, a fact is fiction with pretensions, isn't it? Yes, I am crazy. I know not what I say or think.

And there is more to say, my darling – there always is. (Did I say that? 'Darling'!!! See how you're changing me!) I'm still sitting here, looking at you as you sleep, and listening to the steady rhythm of your breathing. But I too MUST get some sleep!! So now I WILL end this letter and leave it here, addressed to you, then undress and join you in bed and I hope in sleep. And in an hour or so the alarum will ring for you, and maybe you'll kiss me half-awake before you dress and get ready to go back to your nursing responsibilities – I hope so! Then maybe we'll have a quick meal, here – I brought in some bread and cooked sausages and even some vegs and fruit. And then I'll go back to sleep while you go to the Hospital. ANN, I LOVE YOU AND ALWAYS WILL LOVE YOU.

As he stands up, Will's fountain-pen drops to the floor. He slips a sheaf of scrawled pages into a blue folder, which he places carefully at the far end of the desk. Then he looks sharply at Ann, hoping the small sound of the dropped pen hasn't woken her. It hasn't.

Thirty-one

Naked, he comes to her.

The pen is mightier than the sword. - Is it? Really? Surely, Ann, you don't -

She stirs, and smiles, and sighs.

England expects every man to do his duty. - If he knows what his duty is! Do I?

He climbs onto the bed, and lies beside her.

Never in the field of human conflict has so much been owed by so many to so few.

They sleep.

Through the night, bombs will fall on London. Explosions, fires, destruction, death. But, now, in the silence, in the afternoon, they sleep.

… we shall defend our island, whatever the cost may be. We shall fight on the beaches, we shall fight on the landing grounds, we shall fight in the fields and in the streets, we shall fight in the hills; we shall never surrender …

They sleep. They sleep. They sleep.

Thirty-two

'So here you are, busy boozing - what a floozie you are becoming, dear Wife!'

'Dear William, just go and get yourself your pint of Bitter, and then come and sit down beside your ever-loving ever-subservient little Wife. I've been waiting for you' she glanced at her watch 'for twenty minutes. What is your excuse?'

He laughed, sitting down beside her at the bar. 'You will soon be totally out of control, Ann! Don't you know that there's a war on? And that you are a married woman? Two sirens already this afternoon, and probably houses and other buildings bombed in the East End, you could hear the fire-engines and ambulances. People are dying and wounded, and you'll soon be tending to them, of course.'

Then he called softly to the Publican 'What do you think, Tom? Is this the dreaded Blitzkrieg? The Blitz! I think it must be.' Tom shrugged.

'If I should die, think only this -' Will continued softly. 'That there's some corner - And meanwhile, may I order a Scottish pie, or a pie of any nationality, for my dear Wife? Good – and I'll have the same. Followed by two helpings of whatever Sweet is on offer.'

Will paid for their meals as she gazed steadily at him. 'It's Cider' she told him, 'what I'm drinking. I think I'm developing a taste for it. I never really liked Ontario cider, too sweet, and Tom recommended this - "*real* cider" you said, didn't you, Tom? It's great – I could get drunk on it. But' and she lowered her voice 'I have something serious to say, dear Husband. And I want to say it straightaway – it's too important to forget. One of the young surgeons at the Hospital – they sometimes join us nurses in the canteen when we have a break, if there's nothing urgent going on – and he said that what he calls the *real* Battle for Britain is definitely about to start, with a huge all-out bombing attack on London – he said he has indistubitle, oh I can't say that word, *important* inside information from an uncle in the War Office that the all-out German attack will begin on Saturday 24th August, which is *tonight*. Hitler, he said, has lost patience with the British after Churchill persuaded our Government not to respond positively to his offer of peace, "peace in our time", and so now the German Army and Air-force, having defeated and occupied France, are massed just across the Channel, ready to invade. Of course he might be wrong, or exaggerating, but, Will, I do think that there's something in it. You can *feel* that something big is going to happen, the tension is what-do-they-say, *palpable*, and so – I want you to promise me that you'll definitely spend tonight in the Underground Station. I know that you -'

'Yes, I *hate* it, Ann. So enclosed and stuffy and *crowded* - well, usually it is – and dirty and noisy – I never get much sleep, and my pillow and blanket get more and more filthy. So – no -'

'*Please*, Will. Look at me – I'm deadly serious. If you refuse, that could be cause for divorce.'

'Oh, all right, if you insist – and you look so ravishing while bullying me.'

'Good. Thank you.' Ann sighed. 'I wish I wasn't so *tired*. I guess everyone in this pub is tired. And we just have to go on going on. I know we've talked about this before. Everybody has.'

Will was silent. He sipped his beer distractedly.

After a few moments, Ann spoke again, slowly and quietly. 'Will, I have a favour to ask. When you are accepted for training in the RAF, as I'm sure you will be, I want a photo of you in *your* uniform with me in my *nurses'* uniform. Agreed?'

He smiled. 'Actually, I've just heard that I *have* been accepted for training, though probably not in a flying capacity – more likely, for mechanical or other support. And I don't know what sort of uniform, or whether I'd even qualify for one. Funny, I remember being so impressed by uniforms during the First War, when I was just a schoolboy, and it seemed that everywhere one was, on the train or bus or in shops, there were uniformed men. And I thought Dad looked very good in *his* uniform. *Now*, in this War, uniforms have of course appeared everywhere again. But you know what? I think *your* uniform is the best of all because it really means something, something *good*, it signifies total commitment to help the wounded, to save the stricken.' There was a pause.

Then Ann spoke slowly. 'You know something that I really regret, Will? And I wonder if it wasn't a cause of the rift between your Father and me. The last time I saw Davey – I was already nursing my cousin, and of course many other wounded men, and anyway I was exhausted, though that's no excuse. I could see Davey was proud of being in uniform, and it wasn't long before he was sent overseas, but somehow it made me angry, unreasonably angry, that he seemed not only proud of the uniform but somehow glad to be seeing the last of me. That seems a mean reaction now, but I remember it intensely. And no doubt guiltily. And I never saw him again. And I never even had a photograph of him in his uniform – like the one of him above the fireplace in Crab-apple Cottage.'

'Oh, Ann -' He broke off as their meal was delivered.

'And you know' she continued. 'I also remember, with pain, the last time I sat with him under that old apple-tree, the one that, you said, was blown down in a storm later. He had made a bench, and put it under the apple-tree so that you could look down the path, and see Street in the near distance, and then gaze into the far distance – in fact he insisted that you could even see the ocean, the English Channel, on a very clear day, though I never could. But I'm blathering on again, Will, my dear Husband. See what an influence you are having on me! But - do you mind me thinking and talking about your Father like this? To some extent, Davey seems like my first husband, and you my second. Is that insulting? I think it probably is.'

'No, Ann. No, my darling – see, I can *say* "darling" too! But no. Time controls us all, Time gives and then Time takes, and we must find happiness and fulfilment even while Time is busy creating us and ageing us and finally destroying us. That's what I think.'

'Oh. And I see' – Ann was looking at the clock above Tom's head – 'Time is about to eject me from your jocund company. I must go, Will.'

'Yes, and *I* should go and get myself ready for another splendid night of *bonhomie* in the Underground Station, as ordained by you. After, of course, I have dutifully accompanied you to the Hospital.' Then he called out 'Good night to Tom and all – and don't let the bombs burst.'

'Oh, Will, you are incorrigible' Ann told him, smiling. 'That was silly.'

Thirty-three

"We'll meet again, don't know how, don't know when ..."
Will had found a space on the platform.

"Rule, Britannia, Britannia rules the waves."
He pulled his blanket up to his chin, and shifted about, trying to find a comfortable position.

"And did those feet in ancient times ..."
He groaned, then smiled thinly at a young man who had asked if he was 'all right' - "Yes, as much as possible, thank you for asking".

"There'll always be an England ..."
Sleepy, he closed his eyes against the lights, and wished he could close his ears against the raucous singing.

And finally, of course ("Don't *bellow*, don't *bellow*" he instructed the singers silently),
"God save our gracious King, Long live our noble King, God save the King!"

Thirty-four

Will was late. And it was raining. Wet and breathless, he hurried towards the Hospital just as a distant siren started up. In the thickening twilight, he didn't see a new pile of sand-bags near the main entrance, tripped, and fell heavily.

Back on his feet, breathless, he staggered inside. The young nurse sitting behind the main desk looked up, smiled, then said with sudden concern 'Are you all right, Sir?'

'Yes, I think so – I've just fallen over your sand-bags at the entrance and banged my right knee. And destroyed my umbrella. Careless! So many impediments along the pavements now – you have to be extra-extra-careful everywhere. They say, don't they, that many more casualties are being caused in London by the Black-out than by the War. But I'll be all right – thanks for your concern - just my haste and carelessness. But

- My wife – she's a nurse here - she telephoned and left a message asking me to come immediately, so I – is she all right?'

'Oh – yes, she's fine, Sir. Matron told me you'd be coming and I was to guide you to the Canteen. Are you all right to walk there? One of the lifts is out of order, Sir, and Matron said the other one must be reserved for patients and staff.'

They walked slowly and carefully down two flights of stairs, Will in some pain. 'Anyway, here we are, Sir.'

When the nurse pushed open the door, Will saw Ann sitting at a table with two other nurses. As he thanked his guide, one of the nurses rose to welcome him, holding out a hand for him to shake. 'We are so glad you could come, your wife said your shop is quite close. You've probably heard about me, I hope in positive terms - I'm the Matron in your wife's ward, but you can call me Nurse Thomas, and this is Nurse Adams, who is your wife's colleague and friend, and of course you're wondering why you were summoned, aren't you? – well, not exactly summoned - and I'm so glad you could join us.' She stopped to take a breath. 'So please sit down. Do you take sugar in your tea? And please help yourself to sandwiches.'

Ann was smiling gently, but looked rather tense, Will thought. 'Thank you, Nurse Thomas' he said, and sat down heavily beside Ann. He reached for the sandwiches.

'Now, I'll have to go soon,' the Matron continued, 'we're expecting some new patients – from the South, I think, they have terrible casualties down there, in Southampton and Portsmouth and other places the Luftwaffe has been bombing, and some of them need specialized treatment. What dreadful weather we've had, too, the coldest winter on record, they say. And now so sunny and warm, almost hot - But I must get on, so let me explain briefly' and she looked sharply across to Will. 'Of course, it's about your wife, and what she has been offered, a Bursary to study the physical and psychological effects of hospitalization on Children, at the University of Edinburgh - we will be so sorry to lose her, she has proved to be such an excellent nurse, especially of children, they respond so positively to her - and her colleagues have also expressed great appreciation of her kindness and generosity in helping to make it possible for them to be home at night with their children and husbands. Your wife has made it clear that she would like to accept the bursary, but only if you are agreeable, and she is very aware that moving to Edinburgh could be a problem for you, disruptive of your work – you manage a major London shop, I gather. I must report her acceptance or refusal within a few days, so it seemed important to discuss the matter immediately with you both, and she agreed. I hope all that is clear. After you have discussed the matter further, please give me your joint final answer within two days. And now I must go, it was very good to meet you, and I think I can see why Ann married you, if you don't mind my saying so, it's intended of course as a compliment.'

As soon as the Matron had departed, Nurse Adams stood up. 'I must go too, I'll be on duty soon. It's been a great pleasure to meet Ann's husband at last, I can see now why she was keeping him secret – oh, now, I'm joking, but I hope we can get together soon, and with my husband Norman, he'd love to meet you both. See you in the ward, Ann. But no need to rush. '

Will and Ann sat in silence briefly. Then he reached across the table to take her hand. 'So – that was your Gorgon? You must be relieved that she and I didn't come to blows. Even after she implied that I was so inferior to you.'

'Oh, Will. Don't joke about it – we have to make a decision so quickly, and I know it's a serious matter for you as well as me. Even if you're in the RAF. But I told you Matron's not so bad. What do you think, though? About Edinburgh? At least we'd be away from all this bombing. And the constant worrying. And you hate the nights in the Underground.'

'Yes, there's all that. Did you know that London's population now is only half what it was? Because of course so many Londoners have gone off into the countryside, or I expect to relatives or friends in other cities or countries. For the duration, I suppose - or until they can see how things will work out. It'll hardly be worth it for the Nazis to bomb London soon.'

'Oh, Will, don't joke about it. Now that you're nearly forty –'

'"Nearly forty"! Yes, and what about you? I was thinking recently that you *are* forty, isn't that how old you said you were, but you must actually be, what, forty-two? Forty-two! Ah, but why bother about things like that, what do they matter? We love each other, isn't that what matters?'

'So you'll come to Edinburgh with me?'

He stood up abruptly. 'Oh, that wasn't fair! Come over here, Old Lady.' She stood and came round the table to him. He kissed her, then laughed softly. 'Well, all right, you win. You knew you would, didn't you? Yes, I'll come to Edinburgh - if I can, If I'm allowed to, until the RAF calls me up - and I'll get drunk every night, on Scotch, and tak' the low road, and then –'

'I must go, Will' she said. 'I've got a responsible job, you know. And you–'

'And me. Yes, I think I can still hear a siren. Or sirens. Another night in the Underground lies before me. Oh well. What's the date today? But does that matter?'

Thirty-five

It was late-afternoon, and almost dark. But not raining now, thank goodness.

Will, limping, made his way slowly and cautiously along the street; heading for his now-habitual Underground night-shelter. Just be careful, Will, he told himself – so many hazards along the streets of London now!

Sirens continued to wail in the distance. Occasionally people hurried past. He was beginning to feel very weary, when he realized he was about to pass the familiar pub entrance. He stopped, noticing that the door seemed to be slightly ajar. He pushed it, and almost fell forward. Then he became aware that a large dark shape had caught him and was holding him up.

'It's all right, sir, I've got you.'

'Tom, it's you, isn't it?'

'Oh, it's Mr Avery, is it? Are you all right, sir?'

'Yes, thank you, Tom – but could I sit down somewhere and just catch my breath?'

'Of course, sir – just lean on me and we'll go inside – and you can sit at the bar, the way you often do. I was just about to lock the door.'

'Lock the door?'

'Oh, you don't know – you haven't been here for a few nights – the Company has decided to close some pubs – maybe until the War ends – for the duration, as we used to say – we had a few bombs along the street behind – and some people think that old pubs like this one could be death-traps – especially now, sir, with the Blitz – that's what the ARP said, anyway - Now, here's the stool–'

Will sat down carefully in the darkness. 'Thank you, and can I ask another favour? Could you call me 'Will', not 'sir'?'

'Oh, yes, sir, if you prefer. And I'm Tom, you know that. Now, will you drink a pint with me, and I hope you'll help me finish these sandwiches and fish-and-chips, I know you like them – if you haven't already had your supper?' He was lighting a candle.

'Thank you, Tom. And I have a question to ask: How is your son?'

'Oh, you mean my nephew – Trevor?'

'Yes. I hope he found a good position?'

'Oh, now. You wouldn't know, he's in hospital, other side of the River, but my wife – she left yesterday for Coventry, she says we'll be safe there, I'll be joining her and our three little ones tomorrow, we'll be living temporary with her parents, near the Cathedral, they've got a big garage - and I can get a job in one of the pubs nearby – but Trevor, he was very lucky not to be badly wounded, he's what they call concussed – they say he'll be out of hospital soon - he got a job near the Docks, not long before, and a bomb fell right near the building he was working in –'

'I'm glad he's all right, Tom. Please give him my regards.'

'Yes, sir, I will. And he said if there was opportunity I should tell you that he appreciated that you showed him round your shop, he was very impressed by it, but he said he didn't think a job there was for him – too posh, I think that's what he meant – because he has an accent, you know what I mean, Cockney, like me, and he would have to be serving toffs all the time, he said, and – mostly they wouldn't be like you, he said – but also a friend who got him that Docks job told him about it just then.'

'Oh. I'm sorry he felt that, Tom. I don't think you know that I've signed up for the Air Force and will be going for training soon – but when I come back, after the War's over, maybe then – Well, we'll see. Excellent sandwiches and fish-and-chips, Tom! Thank you very much. And of course the beer was – topnotch as always. What a pity there's no – you'll be missing your friends and clients.'

'Yes, I will, sir. But it's only for the duration! Here, let me help you off that stool. And I have forgotten to ask about your wife, Ann - the nurse, have I remembered her name right? A lovely young lady - and very kind.'

'Yes, you have. She's busy nursing tonight – and almost every night. I'll tell her you asked after her, Tom. Thank you.'

They had reached the door. Tom blew out the candle he had been holding. They shook hands. Tom opened the door.

A distant shrieking of sirens; the crumping sounds of distant explosions and gunfire.

Will walked as fast as he dared, towards the Underground station.

Thirty-six

When Will reached the Hospital in mid-afternoon, and limped carefully downstairs to the staff cafeteria, he found Ann already there, and, sitting opposite her, a young surgeon, who looked up wearily from his sandwiches and coffee, and smiled briefly.

'Oh, Will' she said. 'We've only got a few minutes before we have to go back upstairs – for another operation - so time for just a quick chat. This is James, you remember I told you –'

'Yes, I do remember - you told Ann the Blitz would begin near the end of August – and it did – But when will it end? - Must be so many deaths, so many people killed and wounded, even just near here – whole streets of houses and flats and shops bombed in the last few weeks, just rubble and big holes – And our flat - too dangerous to live there, and no water and electricity - So it's good that Ann can be here full-time - or almost - and I can always spend the night in our Haberdashery Department, if it's too dangerous to try to get to the Underground station, and anyway it's so crowded there now, and everything so filthy, and one can hardly breathe - I'm sorry, talking too much – And I didn't even say it's good to meet you, James. Talking too much!'

James: 'Oh, better to talk when we can – mostly there's no time even to think, you just have to do what you have to do, don't you? But, I'm sorry - we don't know each other, Will, but I've heard a bit about you from your wife – whose nursing is so invaluable - we're going to miss her very greatly when she goes on that Edinburgh course. And you run one of those big shops in Oxford Street, don't you - I hope I'm remembering correctly? It's good to meet you.'

'Yes. And so far – well, you probably know that some big West End shops have been destroyed. As you say, we just have to keep on keeping on. Ann has probably told you that I've volunteered – Air Force – But meanwhile, until they summon me for training, I'm helping to keep everything shipshape in that Oxford Street shop, the one you mentioned. And showing my successor, who was in charge of Perishables, the ropes, for when I go. The whole Rationing system that the Government brought in at the beginning of the year is quite demanding for a shop as big as ours – especially when customers need help – many of our older customers, the ones who have had to stay in London whatever happens, are confused and forgetful. And of course, as Ann may have told you, we have increasing problems with deliveries – and some items, like sugar, fruit and even meat are - '

James had been looking at his watch. 'Sorry to interrupt, old boy. I must go – the op is scheduled for four-thirty. Ann can stay a bit longer, but I must leg it, I'm afraid. Good to meet you, and all the best for the future – when this bloody war is over.'

He stood up, and so did Will. They shook hands. Then Will turned to Ann.

She stood up, took his hand and held it. They looked into each other's eyes, steadily.

'Are you sure you're all right?' he asked.

'Oh yes. I think I'm lucky to be able to almost live here now. And as we always say, don't we, you've just said it, we must just carry on and do the best we can. And Will, before you can say it to me, my darling: I love you. Look after yourself. It'll be getting dark out there now, and you're still limping, so be careful –'

'Oh, I will be. My darling Ann, oh my darling. I wish we could have more time together. And I wish - Sometimes I get so - *Après la guerre*, eh? Then we'll be able to make up for all our lost time. And we will.'

Ann smiled. 'Yes, my dear husband.' Will kissed her, and they hugged each other briefly.

Dear Will and Ann,

Im writing this now on the night after you left. Fortune telephoned to say the train was on time – so you would get to London in good time for you to have a good rest Ann before your night duty. I hope you both will take great care in London. I have a feeling – sometimes I think I must be clarevoyant – that soon there will be a very big Nazi attack. We here will know its happening because they fly right over us – or near us anyway - & we can hear explosions. If that happens I hope you will go into a shelter – they say the underground stations are shelters too.

Anyway what I wanted to say is thank you for coming on Sunday. Im sorry you had that disagreement with Roger, Will – he can be very bad tempered - and so can you Will, don't you agree Ann. But I think he regreted it & probably you do too Will. Your Father always hated anger & violence whatever other faults he had. Jane will keep all those letters safe during the War - she promised to do that. I will say only that some of the letters I saw – I only saw a few – did shock me – the ones from Peter Arnold & some other men. I don't know why he kept them – they should have been destroyed – but I also know that men & women behave very differently & we just have to accept that but still we – men as well as women! – should treat each other with kindness & respect. Otherwise we are only animals? Or as I often think, WORSE than animals.

Anyway its getting late & I must go to bed. I just wanted to say to you – you must know this I think – I am so very happy that you both love each other - & will support each other always. How does it go in the Church Service? Yes, "Love, Honour & obey" – well, I don't know about the OBEY, Davey & I were not very good at that – obeying! But we managed - & I know he woud agree with me when I say LOVE EACH OTHER ALWAYS!

I love you both.

Your Mother (Will) and Everlasting Friend (Ann)

P.S. I HOPE YOU WILL BE ABLE TO COME AGAIN SOON.

P.P.S. Sorry I forgot your birthday Will.

ALSO I am sorry this letter is so LATE – I forgot to post it.

Tuesday 17th September, 1940

Dear Mum,

I don't know how to write this. I thought I should phone but I just couldn't. I'm sorry.

Ann was killed in the bombing a few nights ago.

I was late because I needed to check the orders and accounts one more time. I heard the siren when I left the Shop and then I saw thick smoke rising as I walked along the pavement towards the Underground Station. I thought it was from the Docks, which the Luftwaffe have been bombing nearly every night for a while. But as you no doubt know, we here have recently also been having very heavy air-raids night after night and even during the day, with severe destruction and many deaths in various parts of London.

Then suddenly as I was walking towards the Underground, there were fire-engines wailing, and somehow then I knew it was the Hospital, so I ran, or tried to, but when I got near I saw that the whole building was in flames and I couldn't do anything. The fire-engines were pouring water into the building but it was too late. The firemen and ARP were bringing all the patients out that they could. They were crying and screaming.

Mum, I can't say any more. It was horrible and I knew Ann was in there. I hoped she wasn't but I knew she had to be, doing her nursing duties. The whole building was burning and the firemen were shouting at us to stay back.

Please tell Jane and Emily and all the family, I can't, and also I want you all to know that I've signed up now to join the RAF. I won't be a Pilot, too old, but there are other jobs I can do, like Navigator. Anyway, looks as if I will be sent to the Colonies for training ASAP – I think to an aerodrome near a place called Bulawayo in a colony in Africa that I don't think any of us ever heard of, called Southern Rhodesia. But there are training aerodromes all over the Empire now.

I'll write later, when I can. Just at the moment – well, you can guess how I'm feeling, maybe, Mum. Confused and I think in mourning. I don't know how I can ever – Ann was such a lovely person. You know that, and you know how much I love her. I can't write any more at the moment, and I hope this letter reaches you safely.

Look after yourselves. Please give my love to Jane and Emily and the boys – and keep some love for yourself.

Will

Acknowledgements

Several texts influenced the evolution of this novel, notably the three volumes of Vera Brittain's major Diaries published by Victor Gollancz: *Chronicle of Youth, War Diary 1913–1917* (ed. Alan Bishop); *Chronicle of Friendship, Diary of the Thirties 1932–1939* (ed. Alan Bishop); and especially *Wartime Chronicle, Diary 1939–1945* (ed. Alan Bishop and Y. Aleksandra Bennett); as well as *Testament of a Generation: The Journalism of Vera Brittain and Winifred Holtby* (ed. Paul Berry and Alan Bishop); and *Letters from a Lost Generation: First World War Letters of Vera Brittain and Four Friends* (ed. Alan Bishop and Mark Bostridge).

Other texts also provided helpful information, among them: Vera Brittain, *England's Hour*; Vera Brittain, *Testament of a Peace Lover* (ed. Winifred and Alan Eden-Green); Paul Hastings, *Between the Wars, 1919–1939*; Bernard Bergonzi, *Wartime and Aftermath*; A.J.P. Taylor, *The Second World War*; R.A.C. Parker, *Struggle for Survival*; Peter Calvocoressi, Guy Wint and John Pritchard, *The Causes and Courses of the Second World War*, Volume 1; Michael Clark and Peter Teed, *The Twentieth Century, 1906–1960*; *Second World War Poems* (ed. Hugh Haughton); Edward Bishop, *Their Finest Hour: The Story of the Battle of Britain 1940*; Leslie F. Hannon, *Canada at War*.

I am grateful for the patient support of my wife Judith, the stimulation of the literary group in Cayuga, and the kind efficiency of my publisher David Stover.

About the Author

Peter Abbot is the author of several novels and novellas, including *Librarian* (2016), *Gukurahundi: Voice of the Lord* (2018), and *Hamiltonians* (2018). He lives and writes in Hamilton, Ontario.